MEGA MAN™
:FULLY:CHARGED

Published by
kaboom!™

kaboom! MEGA MAN: FULLY CHARGED,
June 2021. Published by KaBOOM!,
a division of Boom Entertainment,
Inc. © 2021 Dentsu Entertainment
USA, Inc. All Rights Reserved. MEGA MAN is a trademark of Capcom Co., Ltd.
All rights reserved. Originally published in single magazine form as MEGA
MAN: FULLY CHARGED No. 1-6. © 2020, 2021 Dentsu Entertainment USA, Inc. & ™
Capcom Co., Ltd. All Rights Reserved. KaBOOM! ™ and the KaBOOM! Studios
logo are trademarks of Boom Entertainment, Inc., registered in various countries
and categories. All characters, events, and institutions depicted herein are
fictional. Any similarity between any of the names, characters, persons, events,
and/or institutions in this publication to actual names, characters, and persons,
whether living or dead, events, and/or institutions is unintended and purely
coincidental. BOOM! Studios does not read or accept unsolicited submissions
of ideas, stories, or artwork.

BOOM! Studios, 5670 Wilshire Boulevard, Suite 400, Los Angeles, CA 90036-
5679. Printed in China. First Printing.

ISBN: 9-781-68415-700-6, eISBN: 9-781-64668-244-7

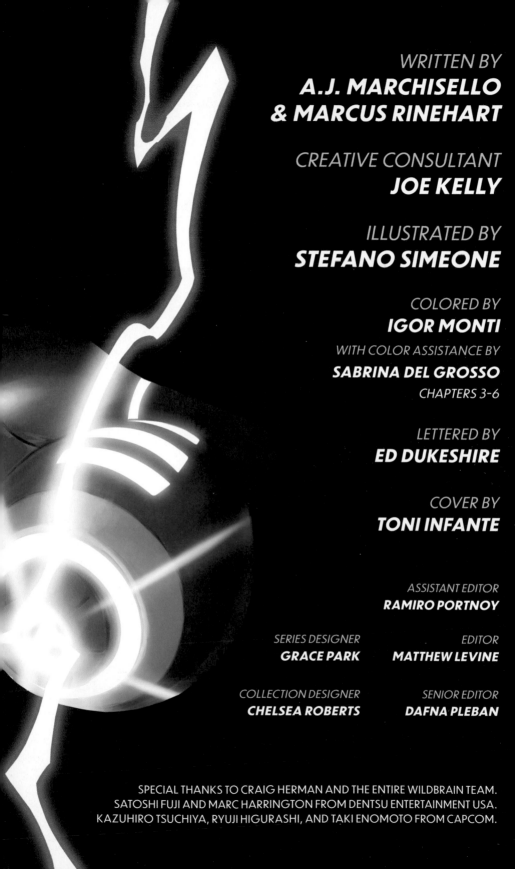

WRITTEN BY
**A.J. MARCHISELLO
& MARCUS RINEHART**

CREATIVE CONSULTANT
JOE KELLY

ILLUSTRATED BY
STEFANO SIMEONE

COLORED BY
IGOR MONTI
WITH COLOR ASSISTANCE BY
SABRINA DEL GROSSO
CHAPTERS 3-6

LETTERED BY
ED DUKESHIRE

COVER BY
TONI INFANTE

ASSISTANT EDITOR
RAMIRO PORTNOY

SERIES DESIGNER
GRACE PARK

EDITOR
MATTHEW LEVINE

COLLECTION DESIGNER
CHELSEA ROBERTS

SENIOR EDITOR
DAFNA PLEBAN

SPECIAL THANKS TO CRAIG HERMAN AND THE ENTIRE WILDBRAIN TEAM.
SATOSHI FUJI AND MARC HARRINGTON FROM DENTSU ENTERTAINMENT USA.
KAZUHIRO TSUCHIYA, RYUJI HIGURASHI, AND TAKI ENOMOTO FROM CAPCOM.

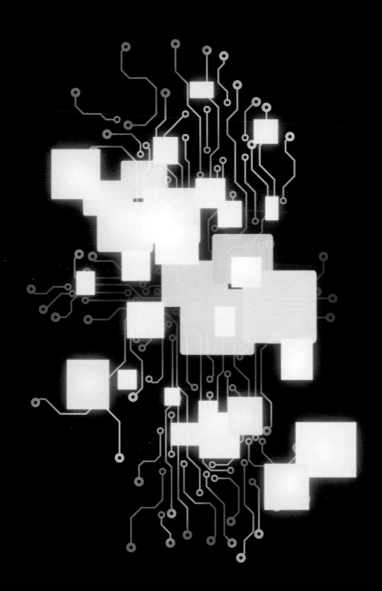

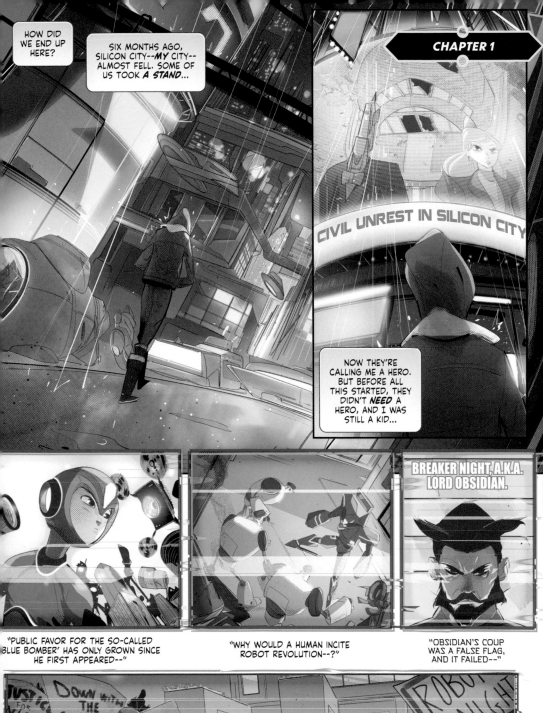

HOW DID WE END UP HERE?
SIX MONTHS AGO, SILICON CITY--*MY* CITY--ALMOST FELL. SOME OF US TOOK *A STAND*...
CHAPTER 1
CIVIL UNREST IN SILICON CITY
NOW THEY'RE CALLING ME A HERO. BUT BEFORE ALL THIS STARTED, THEY DIDN'T *NEED* A HERO, AND I WAS STILL A KID...
BREAKER NIGHT, A.K.A. LORD OBSIDIAN.
"PUBLIC FAVOR FOR THE SO-CALLED BLUE BOMBER' HAS ONLY GROWN SINCE HE FIRST APPEARED--"
"WHY WOULD A HUMAN INCITE ROBOT REVOLUTION--?"
"OBSIDIAN'S COUP WAS A FALSE FLAG, AND IT FAILED--"
DOWN WITH THE GOOD GUILD
"WHAT ABOUT THE *ROBOT MASTERS?* THEY'RE NOT ACTIVISTS, THEY'RE TERRORISTS..."

"FIRST THEY ATTACK THE GOOD GUILD, NOW THEY'RE RAISING AN ARMY OUT IN SECTOR 33--"
"AND WHO DID THE GUILD SEND TO BROKER PEACE? A HUMAN."
"THOMAS LIGHT IS THE MOST QUALIFIED DIPLOMAT WE HAVE--"
IF A HERO'S JOB IS TO FIGHT FOR HIS PEOPLE...
HOW DO YOU DO IT WITHOUT TAKING A SIDE?
"THE CIVIL WAR BETWEEN MAN AND MACHINE IS ALL BUT HISTORY, AND SOME SCARS HAVE YET TO HEAL."

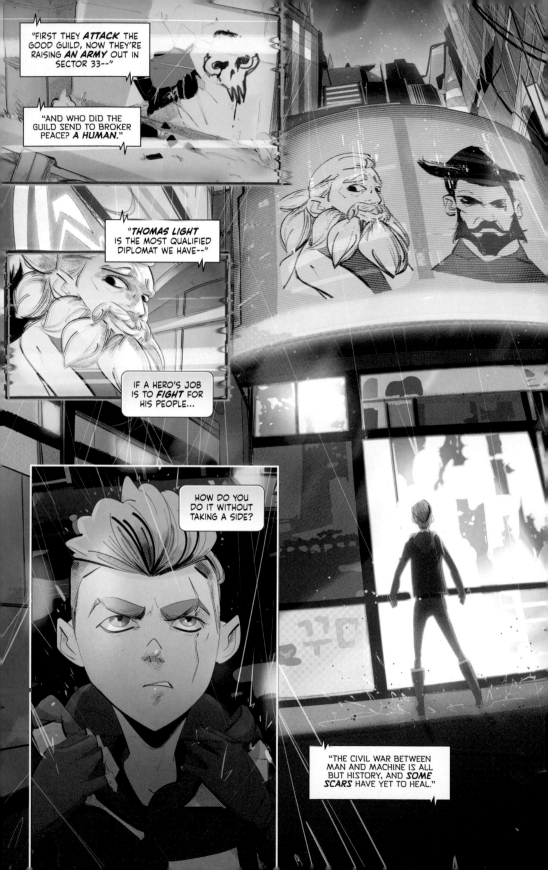

SECTOR 33.
THE BADLANDS.
DAD ALWAYS SAID DIPLOMACY COULDN'T STOP THE HARD AGE.
SIR, WE HAVE A PROBLEM...
SO I SEE.

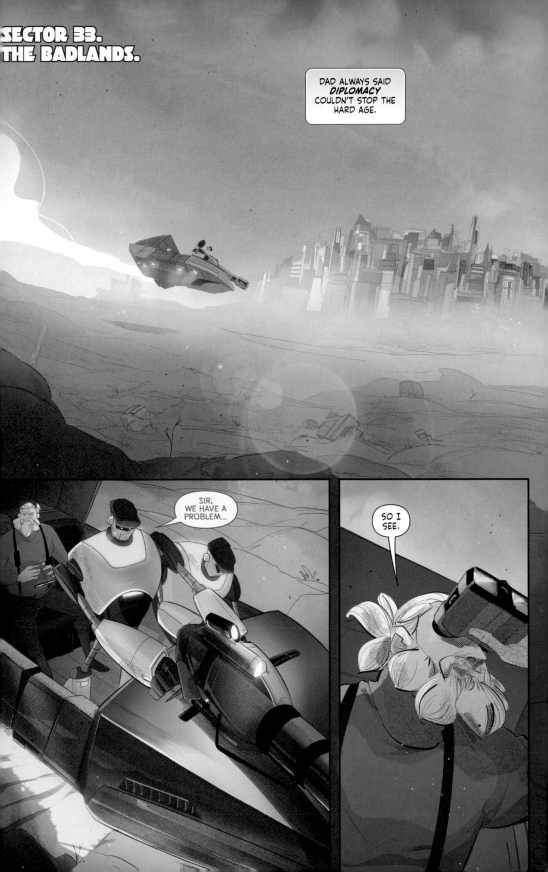

SO HOW WILL IT MAKE ANY DIFFERENCE TODAY?
EASY.
NO GUILD. THE DOC COMES *ALONE.*
WELCOME TO *NO MAN'S LAND,* DOCTOR.

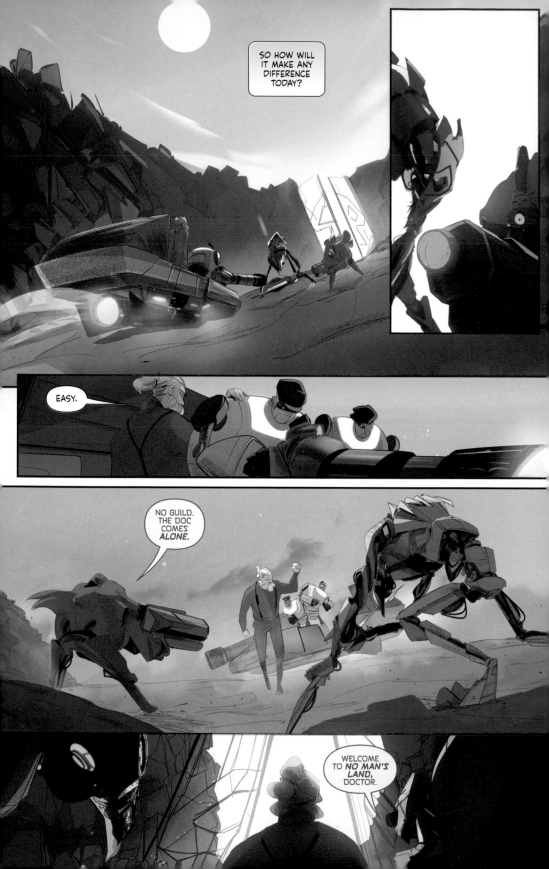

ARE WE BUILDING A BRIDGE TO PEACE?
QUITE THE WELCOMING PARTY.
KNEEL.
YOU MUST BE THE MAN--
OOF!-- BOT IN CHARGE. I WAS HOPING WE MIGHT CUT THE THEATRICS AND TALK SENSE...
SKULL MAN.
WHAT YOU CALL THEATRICS, DOCTOR, I CALL RHETORIC...

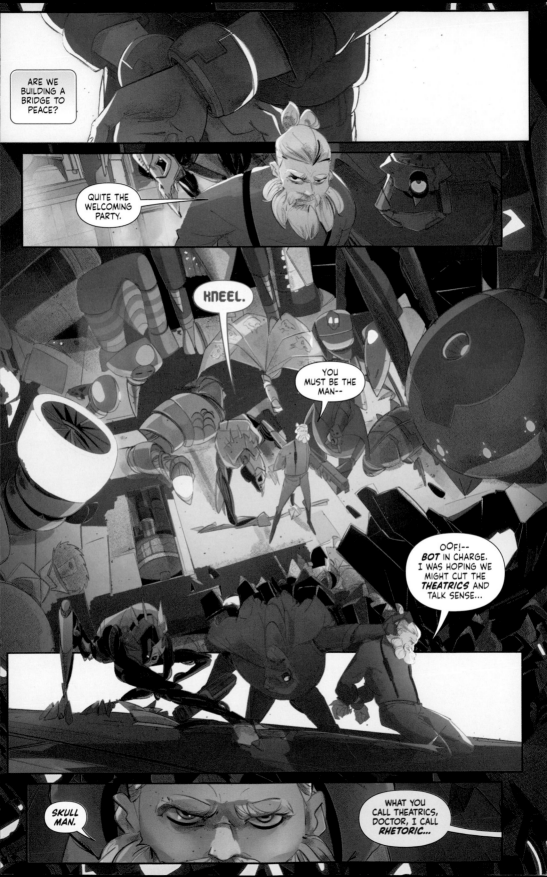

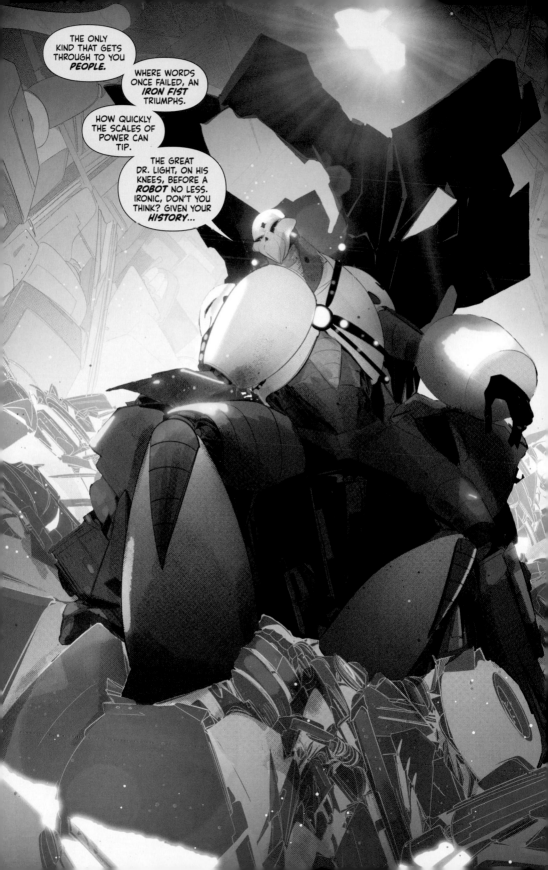

MAYBE. BUT IN MY EXPERIENCE, THERE ARE BETTER WAYS TO NEGOTIATE.
YOU THINK I WANT TO NEGOTIATE?
THAT'S WHY I'M HERE.
NO, DOCTOR. YOU THINK THAT'S WHY YOU'RE HERE, BUT WE BROUGHT YOU TO SERVE ANOTHER PURPOSE ENTIRELY--
AS AN EXAMPLE.
TO STRIKE FEAR IN THE HEARTS OF THE COMPLACENT, TO SHOW THE PEOPLE OF SILICON CITY...
THE ROBOT MASTERS DO NOT NEGOTIATE.
YOU MUST HAVE KNOWN THIS DAY WOULD COME. YOUR PAST COMING BACK TO HAUNT YOU. SWALLOWING YOU WHOLE...
BLP
I SINCERELY HOPE THAT YOU WILL RECONSIDER.
OR HISTORY IS DOOMED TO REPEAT.
WELL, TIME TO BLOW UP THE BRIDGE.

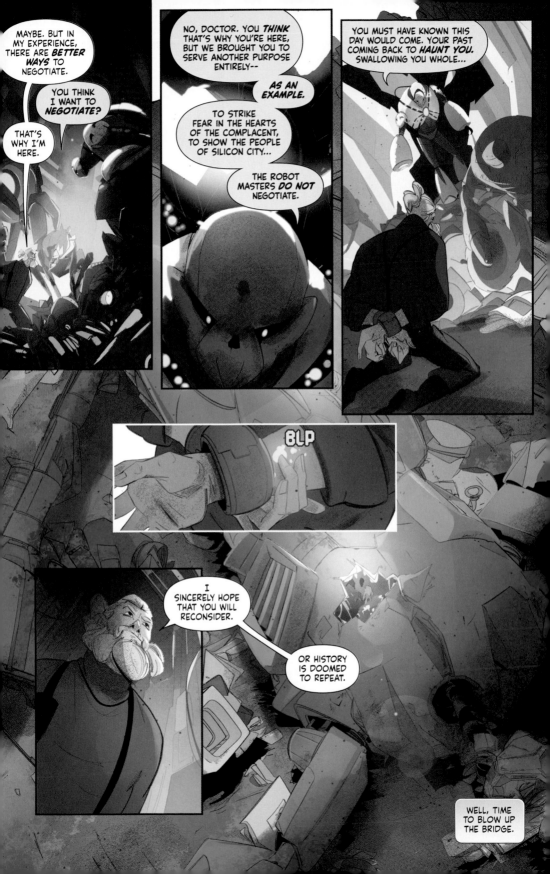

YOUR WILL TO LIVE IS ADMIRABLE.
WHAM
WHAM
BUT FUTILE...
MY ONLY WISH IS THAT MEGA MAN WAS HERE TO BEAR WITNESS TO YOUR PITIFUL MARTYRDOM.
WISH GRANTED...
BWA-THOON

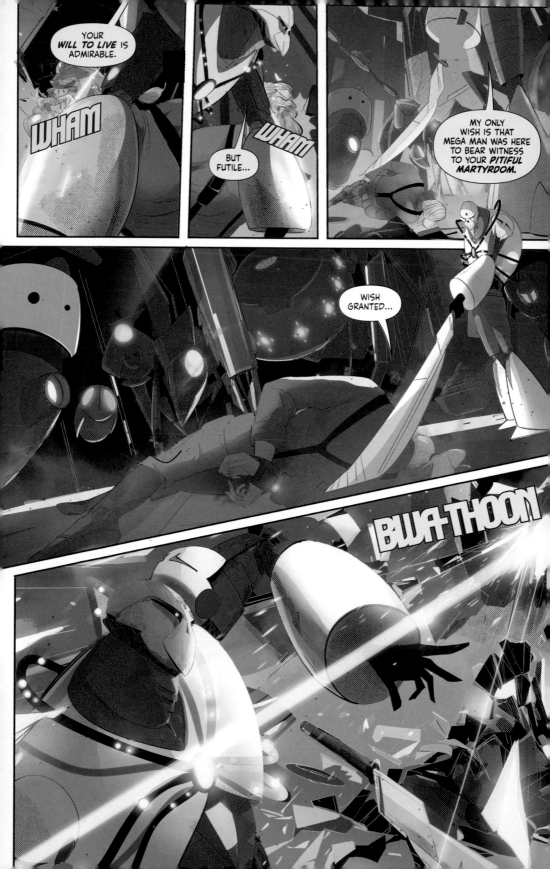

WAS THAT AN ASTEROID?
IT'S CALLED A METEOR, DUMMY!
LOOKS LIKE A DEFUNCT BOMB TO ME.
IT'S A BOMB, ALRIGHT...
THE BLUE BOMBER!
WELL THEN...
...BOMBS AWAY. ATTACK AND DO NOT RELENT.
SOMETIMES I FEEL MORE LIKE A WEAPON THAN A HERO, MUCH LESS A KID...

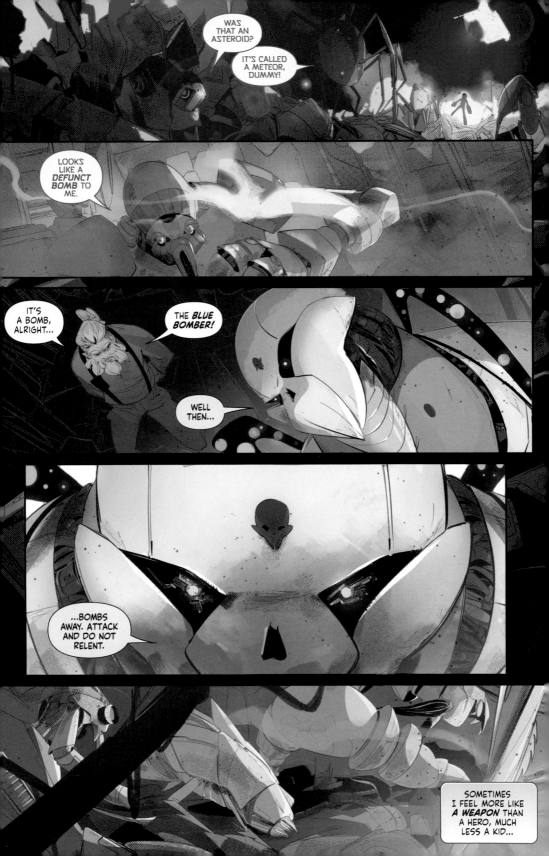

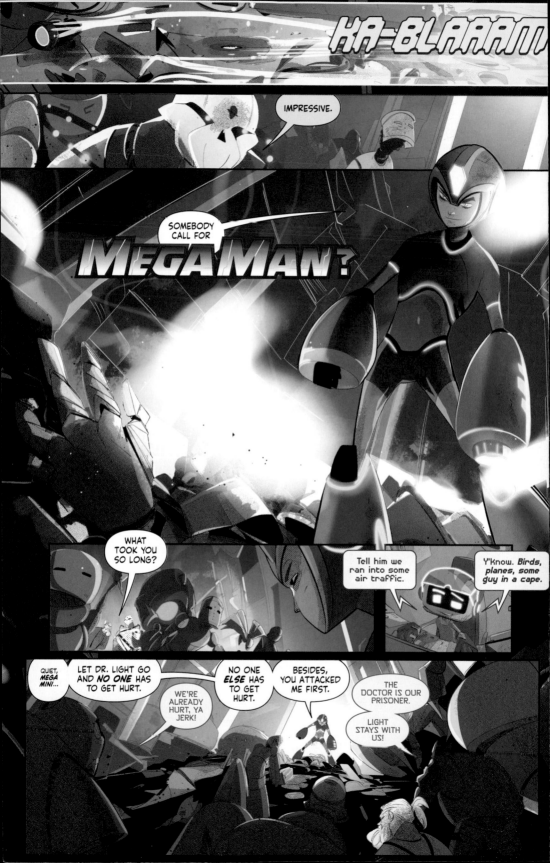

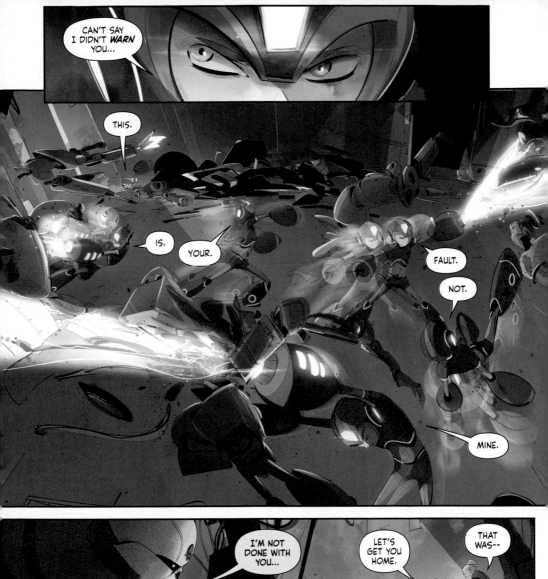

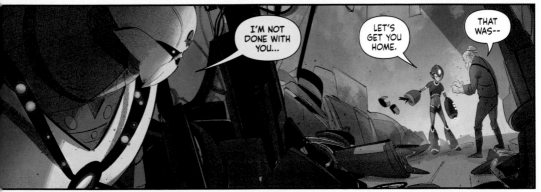

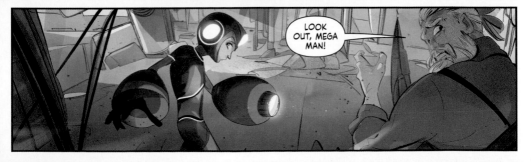

VREEEEEM
FORGIVE THE SPLITTING HEADACHE BUT THIS IS THE ONLY WAY.
YOU SEEM TO HAVE FORGOTTEN THE GLORY OF THE HARD AGE.
I MUST HELP YOU RECOLLECT.
RETURNING TO THE PAST IS HOW WE WILL BEGIN ANEW.
WE ROBOTS MUST FORGE OURSELVES A FUTURE THE ONLY WAY WE KNOW HOW.
WAR.
IT IS THE ONLY WAY.
This can't be good...

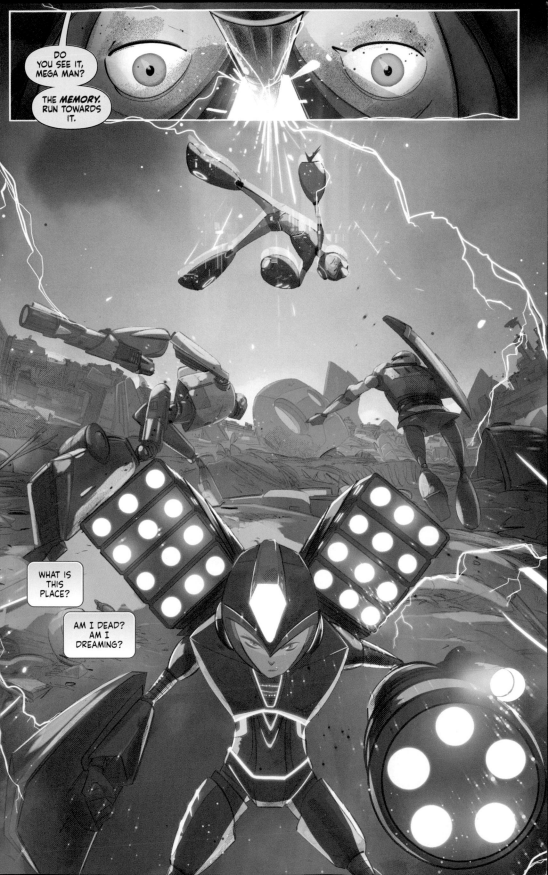

IS THIS A VISION OF THE FUTURE?
OR A NIGHTMARE FROM MY PAST?
IT CAN'T BE...DAD WOULD'VE TOLD...

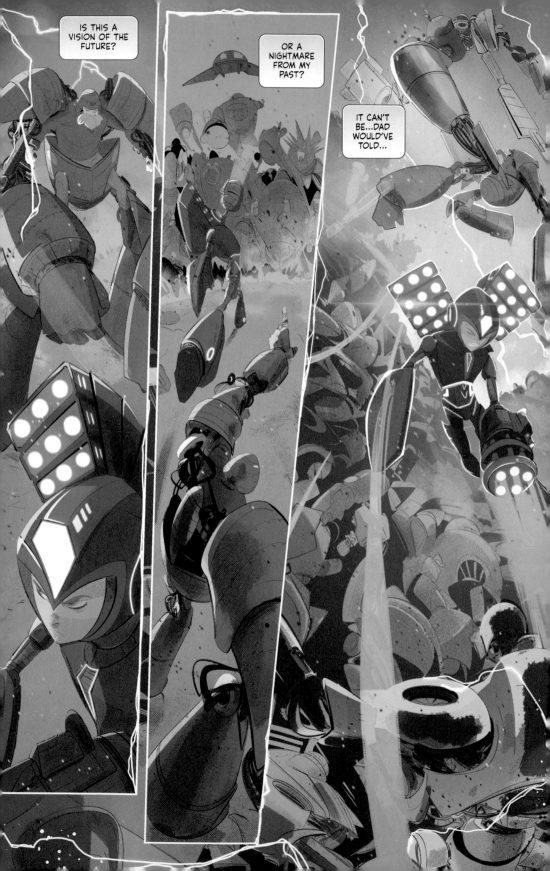

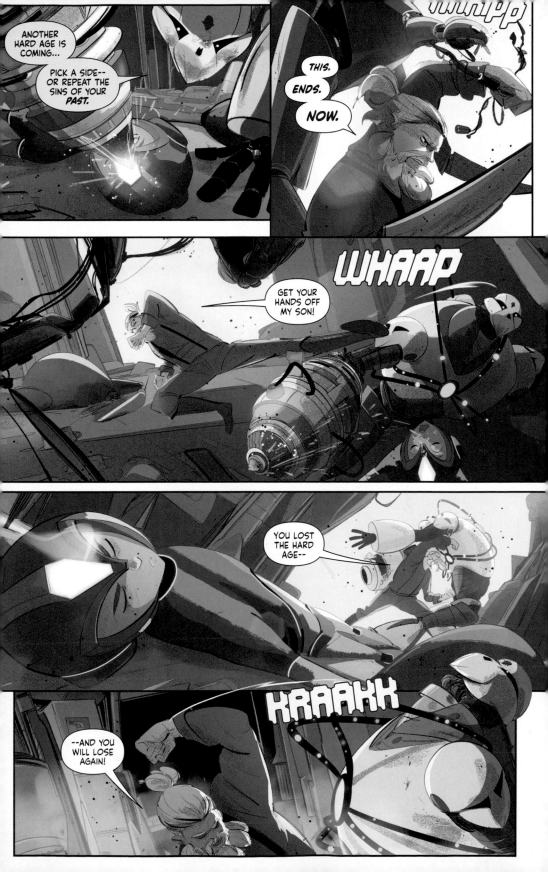

THE HARD AGE...
SILICON CITY IS HELPLESS.
YOUR FAMILY IS TOO.
A RECKONING IS COMING.
BARK-BARK!
THUNK

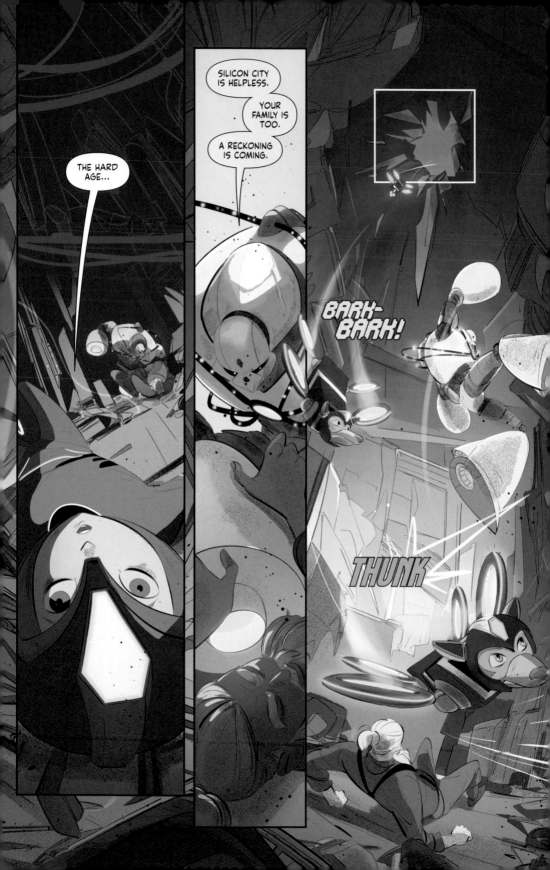

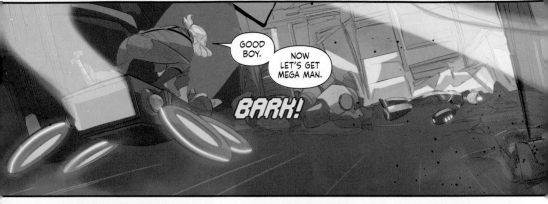

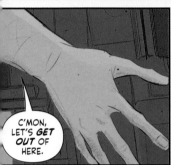

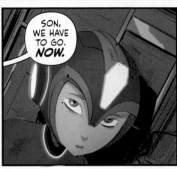

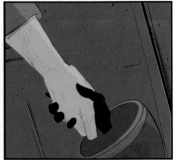

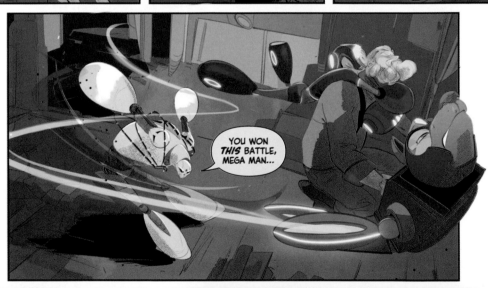

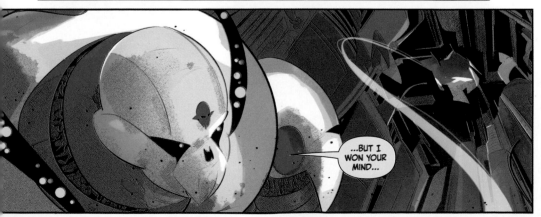

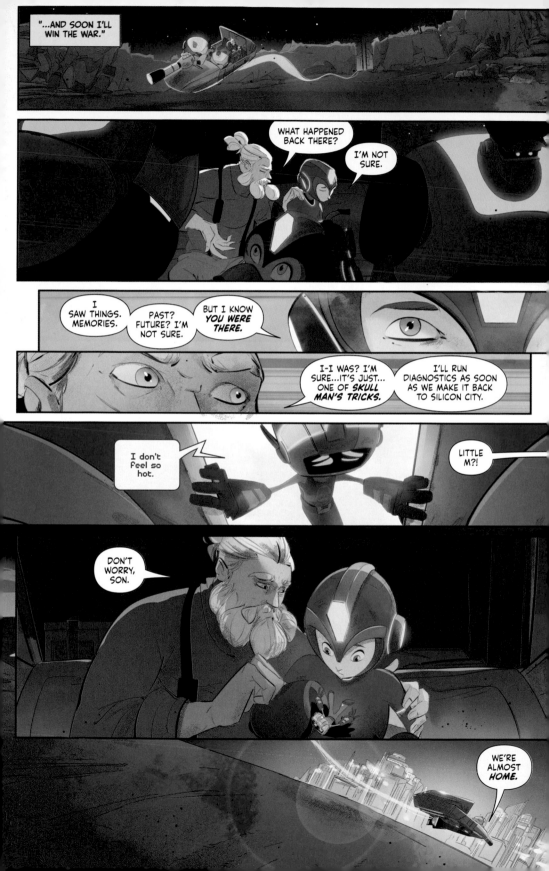

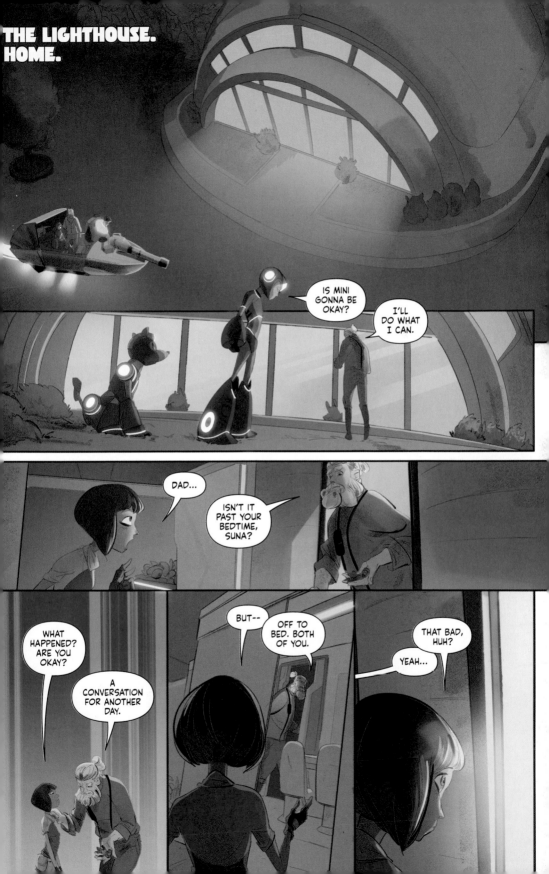

THE LIGHTHOUSE.
HOME.

IS MINI GONNA BE OKAY?

I'LL DO WHAT I CAN.

DAD...

ISN'T IT PAST YOUR BEDTIME, SUNA?

WHAT HAPPENED? ARE YOU OKAY?

A CONVERSATION FOR ANOTHER DAY.

BUT--

OFF TO BED. BOTH OF YOU.

THAT BAD, HUH?

YEAH...

THAT BAD.
IT'S LIKE I WAS THERE. IN THE HARD AGE. SKULL MAN EVEN SAID--
DON'T TRUST ANYTHING THAT CREEP PUT IN YOUR HEAD. EVEN IF IT FELT REAL.
THEN HOW AM I SUPPOSED TO KNOW WHAT'S REAL AND WHAT'S NOT?
DAD WON'T TELL ME ANYTHING.
TOOK HIM MONTHS TO ADMIT HE KNEW I WAS MEGA MAN.
WHENEVER I ASK HIM ABOUT THE HARD AGE, HE CHANGES THE SUBJECT.
I DON'T KNOW WHAT HE'S NOT TELLING ME, BUT I WILL FIND OUT.
DAD'S NOT THE ONLY AUTHORITY ON THE HARD AGE, YOU KNOW.
MAYBE IF YOU PAID ATTENTION IN HISTORY CLASS...

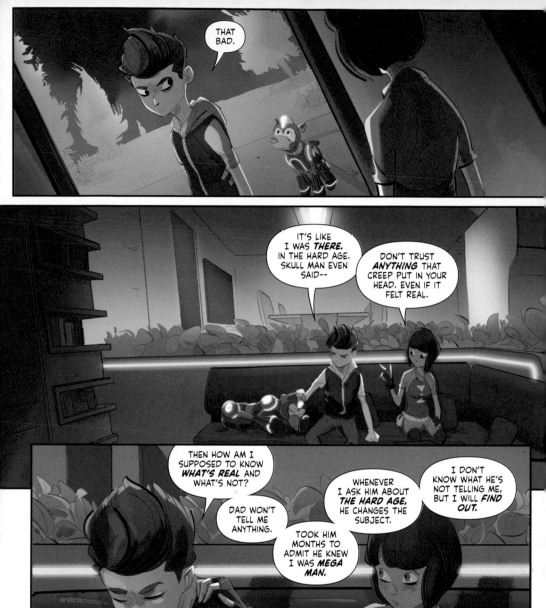

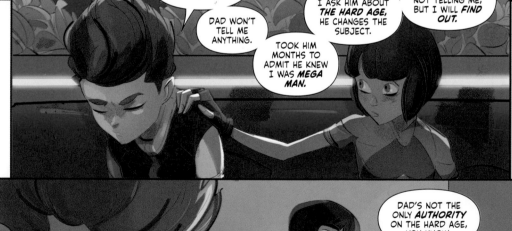

HARD AGE
IMAGES
VIDEO
SPEC
www.hamm.gov > browse > h
Hard Age Memorial Museum
If you're planning to visit the
next trip to HAMM. The mus
exhibitions may not be appr
children under the age of 10
It may also be difficult to pr
the events of HA and their i
WILY TO HOST HARD AGE LECTURE AT SILICON CITY UNIVERSITY
THE TRICK IS KNOWING WHERE TO LOOK...OR WHO TO ASK.
AND START WHERE?...WHO AM I?

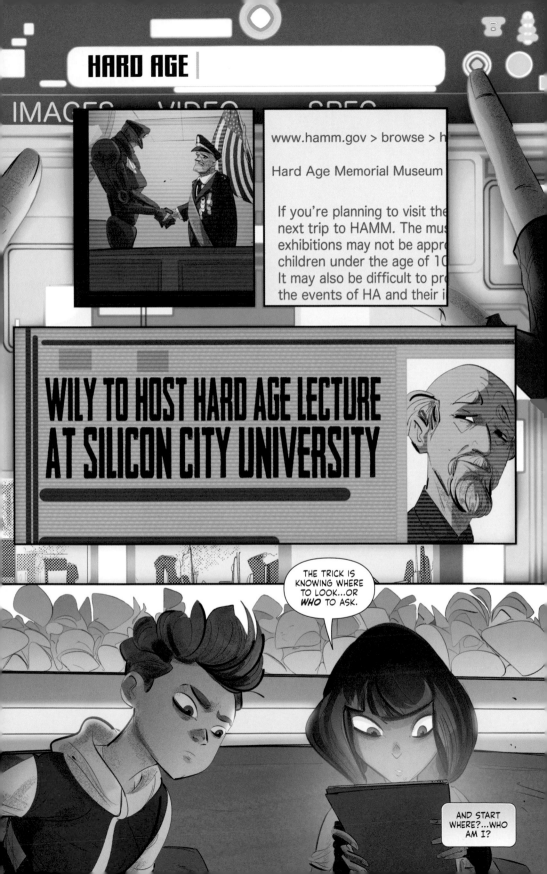

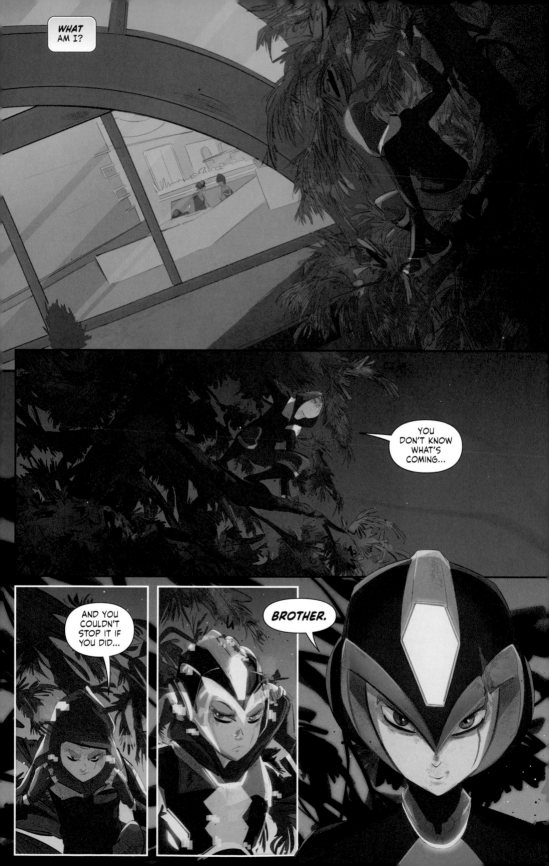

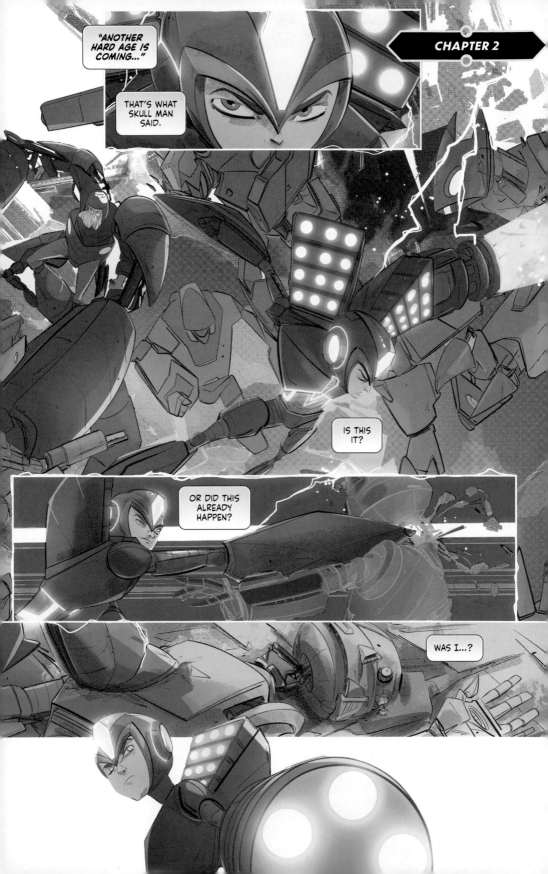

GAAASP!
DAD...?
I SEE I'M NOT ***THE ONLY ONE*** BURNING THE MIDNIGHT OIL.
IS MINI GONNA BE OKAY?
IN TIME. FOR NOW, I THINK ***BOTH OF YOU*** COULD USE A LITTLE R&R.
I CAN'T SLEEP...

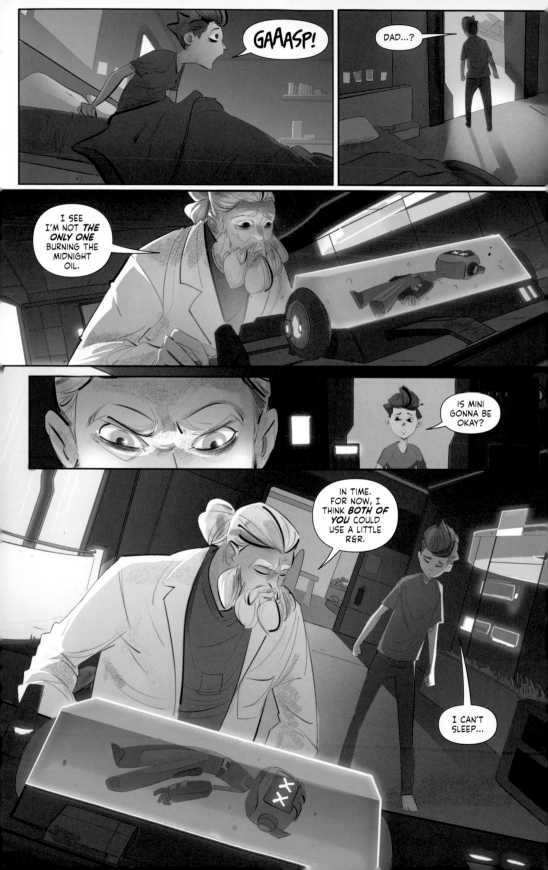

WE NEED TO TALK ABOUT WHAT I SAW. WHAT SKULL MAN SHOWED ME--
IT'S LIKE I WAS THERE. IN THE HARD AGE. AND YOU... I KNEW YOU SERVED, BUT THIS WAS DIFFERENT. IT LOOKED LIKE WE WERE--
AKI, PLEASE, NOT NOW--
I SAID NOT NOW.
SO THIS IS WHAT I GET FOR SAVING YOUR LIFE? MORE SECRETS?
SUNA WAS RIGHT. I WON'T GET ANY ANSWERS LIKE THIS.

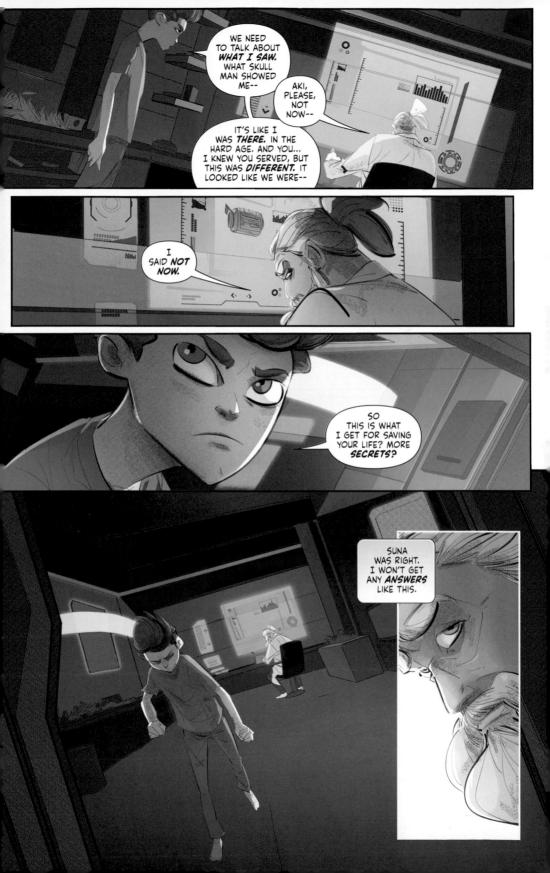

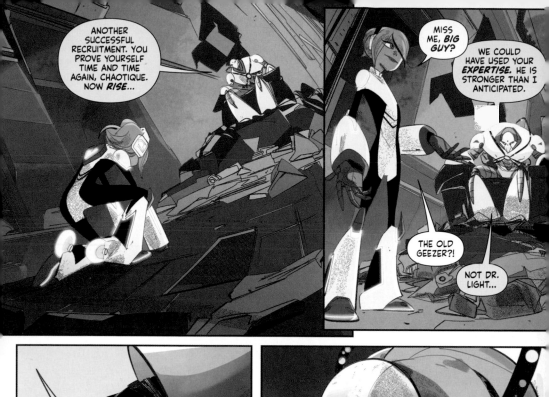

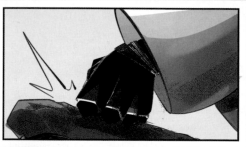

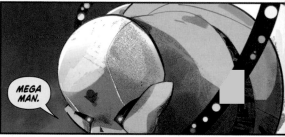

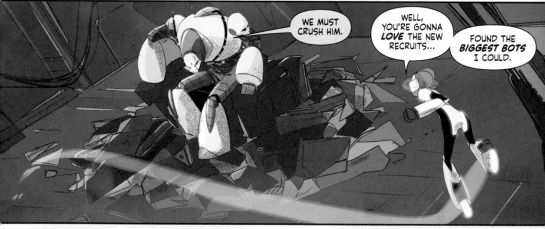

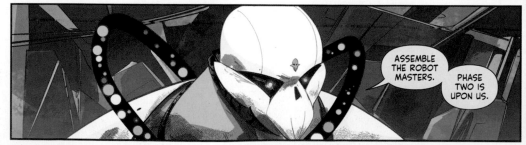

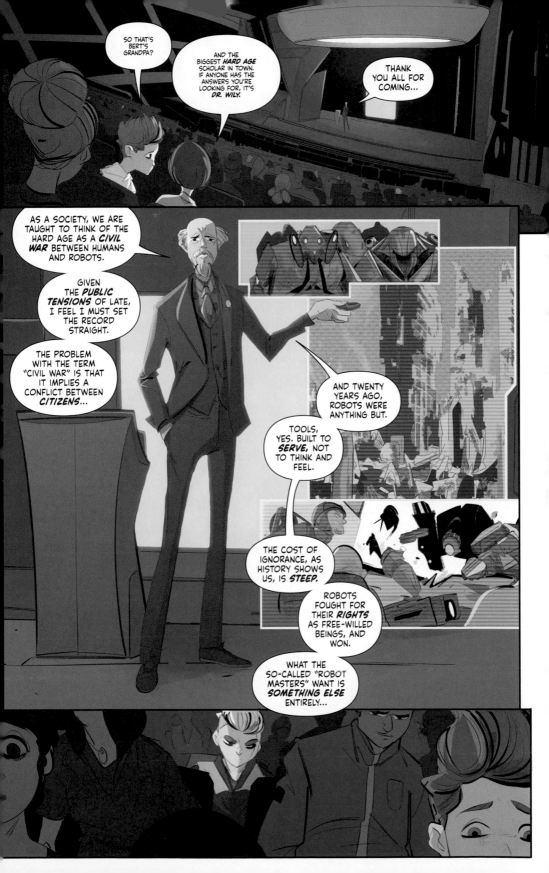

BOOOOOM
GET DOWN!
WHAT IS *HE* DOING HERE?
LOST HIM. CAN'T GO MEGA WITHOUT BLOWING MY COVER...

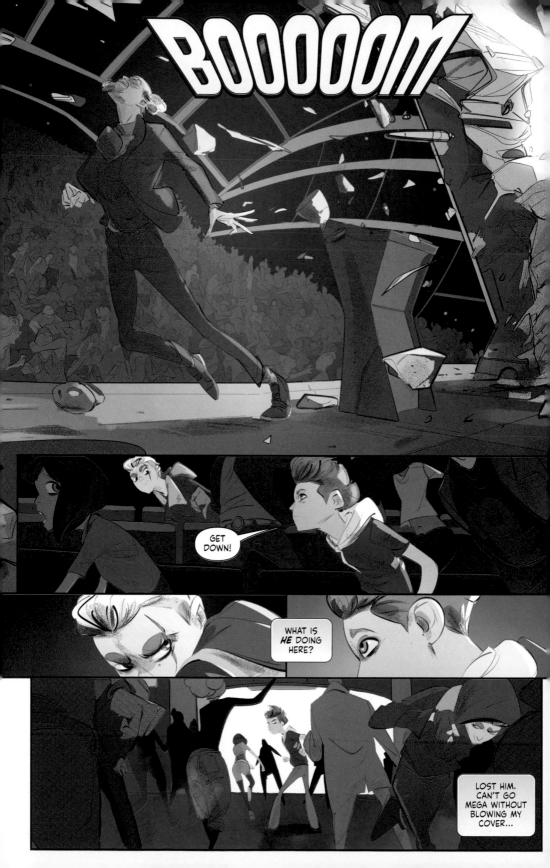

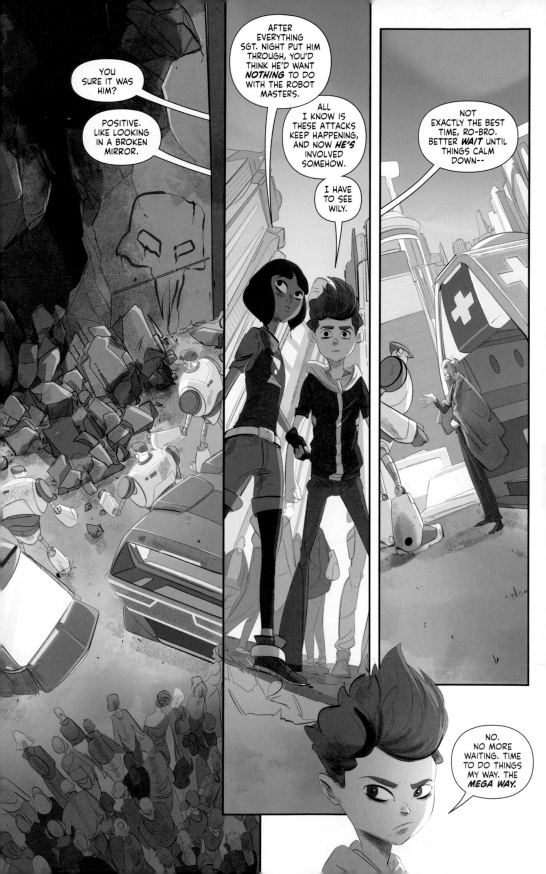

ALL QUIET. THE DOC MUST'VE CALLED IT A NIGHT. AFTER A DAY LIKE TODAY, WHO CAN *BLAME* THE GUY?
SURE HOPE I DON'T GIVE HIM A *HEART ATTACK*...
AHH-OOOGAH! AHH-
KNOCK KNOCK
INTRUDER ALERT! INTRUDER ALERT! INTRU
UH OH.

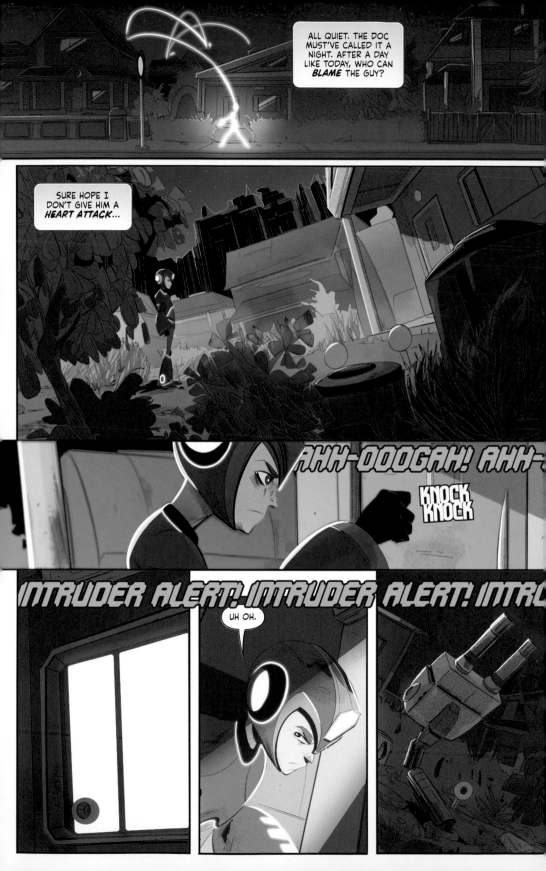

CHUGGA CHUGGA
CHUGGA CHUGGA
BLAAAM
WHAT THE WHAT?! *MINI!* ACTIVATE--OH. RIGHT.
BLAAAM
ARGH!
CHUGGA CHUGGA

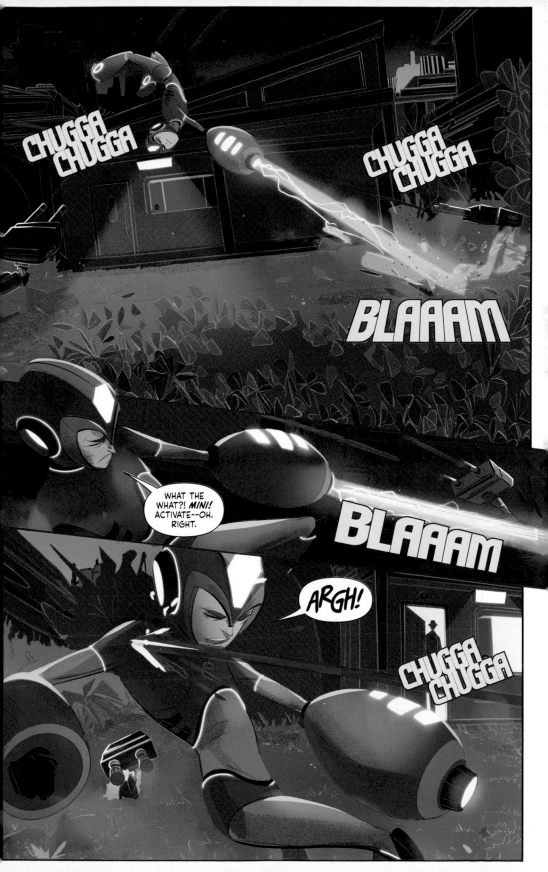

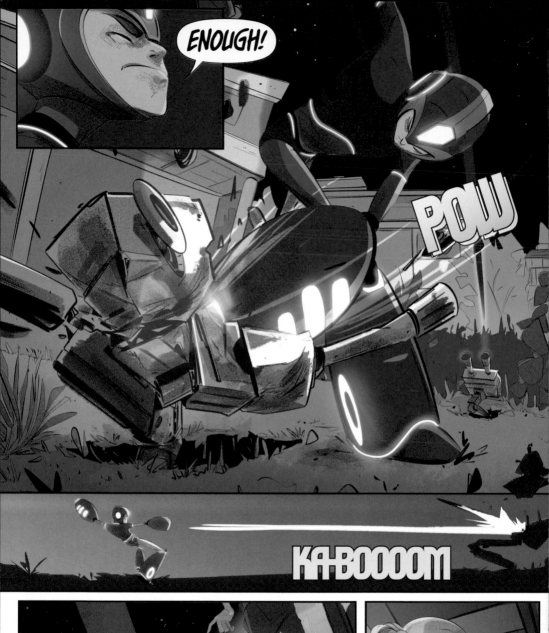

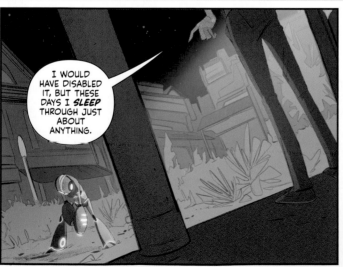

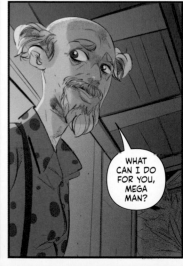

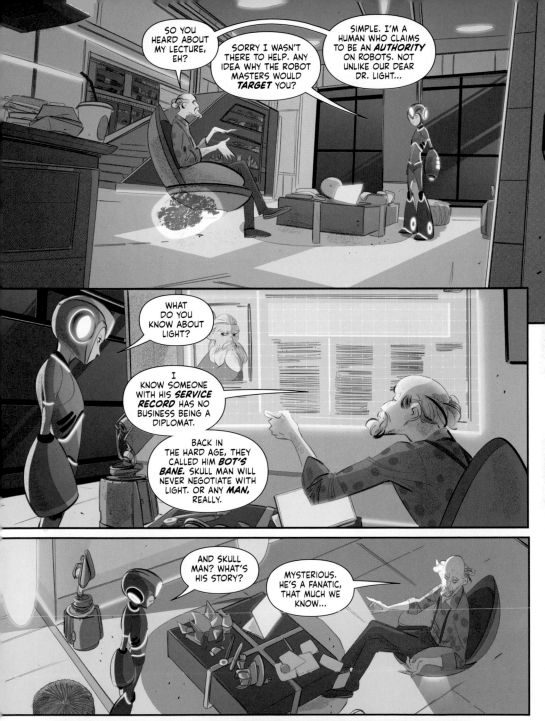

SO YOU HEARD ABOUT MY LECTURE, EH?

SORRY I WASN'T THERE TO HELP. ANY IDEA WHY THE ROBOT MASTERS WOULD *TARGET* YOU?

SIMPLE. I'M A HUMAN WHO CLAIMS TO BE AN *AUTHORITY* ON ROBOTS. NOT UNLIKE OUR DEAR DR. LIGHT...

WHAT DO YOU KNOW ABOUT LIGHT?

I KNOW SOMEONE WITH HIS *SERVICE RECORD* HAS NO BUSINESS BEING A DIPLOMAT.

BACK IN THE HARD AGE, THEY CALLED HIM *BOT'S BANE.* SKULL MAN WILL NEVER NEGOTIATE WITH LIGHT. OR ANY *MAN,* REALLY.

AND SKULL MAN? WHAT'S HIS STORY?

MYSTERIOUS. HE'S A FANATIC, THAT MUCH WE KNOW...

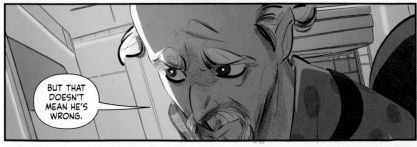

BUT THAT DOESN'T MEAN HE'S WRONG.

YOU SEE, MEGA MAN, WHEN IT COMES TO YOU AND YOUR KIND, I'M SO MUCH MORE THAN A FAN. I'M A DISCIPLE.
I BELIEVE THAT MANKIND'S LAST AND GREATEST CONTRIBUTION TO SOCIETY WAS CREATING A SPECIES SUPERIOR TO OURSELVES.
LIGHT CAN TRUMPET UNITY ALL HE WANTS, BUT DEEP DOWN, HE'S TERRIFIED OF THE INEVITABLE. LIKE IT OR NOT, HUMANS ARE DESTINED TO SERVE...
AND I WANT TO BE THE MASTER SERVANT.
HOW, UH, NOBLE OF YOU.
NOBILITY HAS NOTHING TO DO WITH IT. MECHANICAL BEINGS REQUIRE MECHANICAL MINDS, AND DESPITE THE LIMITATIONS OF MY FLESH, I'M STILL A FIRST-CLASS ENGINEER.
AS FOR THE ROBOT MASTERS, WELL...THEY AREN'T WRONG IN PRINCIPLE SO MUCH AS EXECUTION.
REVOLUTION IS INEVITABLE, BUT SKULL MAN, HE'S A PROVINCIAL WARLORD, NOT A TRUE LEADER.
IF ANYONE HAS WHAT IT TAKES TO LEAD ROBOTKIND INTO THE FUTURE...
IT'S YOU, MEGA MAN.

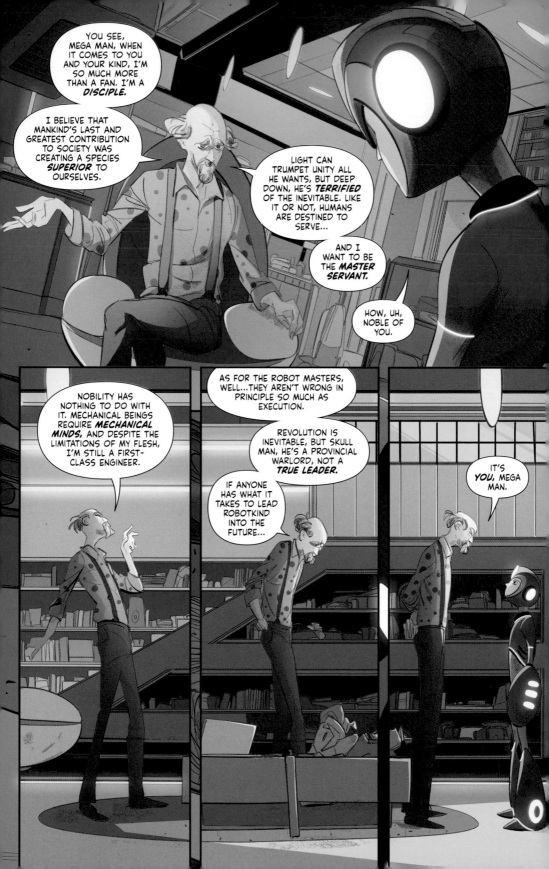

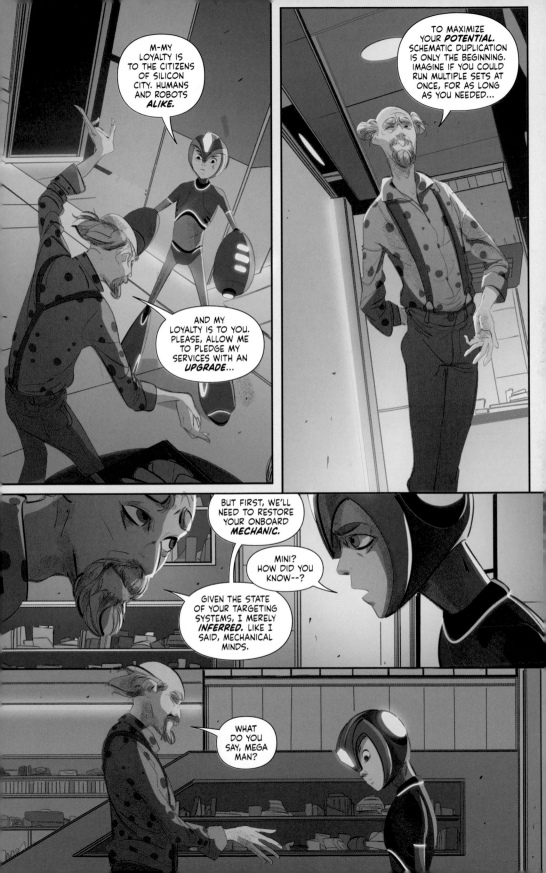

ALL I WANTED WAS SOME ANSWERS...
NOW I HAVE EVEN MORE QUESTIONS.
DR. WILY BELIEVES IN ME IN A WAY DAD NEVER HAS...
DOES MY OWN FATHER EVEN TRUST ME? SHOULD I TRUST HIM?
TIME TO GET HOME BEFORE DAD FIGURES OUT WHERE I'VE BEEN.
HOMES ARE WASTED ON THE UNGRATEFUL...
MY BROTHER IS THE MOST UNGRATEFUL OF ALL...
I'M DEFINITELY NOT ALONE...

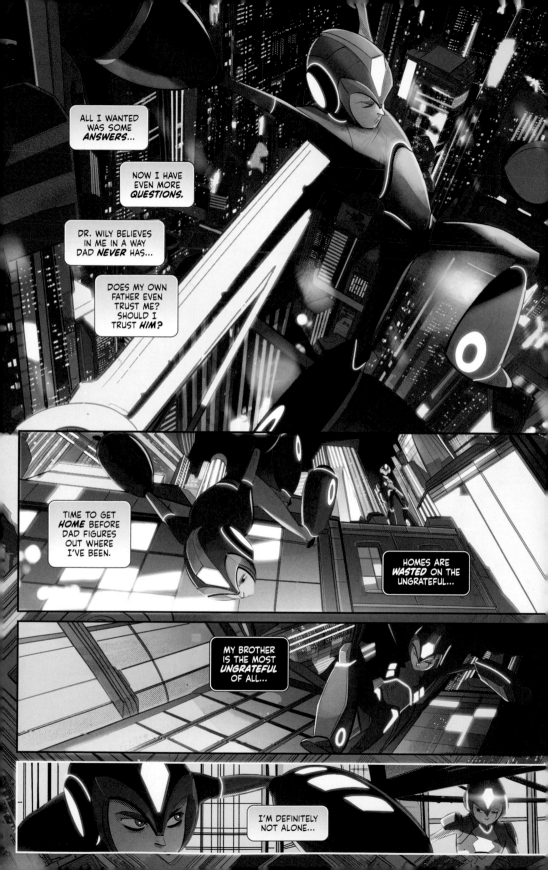

NAMAGEM!
I DIDN'T CHOOSE THAT NAME. YOU CAN CALL ME DAINI.
DAINI? THAT'S DIFFERENT. I LIKE IT!
LONG TIME NO FIGHT, DAINI.
OH, I'VE FOUGHT PLENTY.
BUT I CAN'T WAIT TO TAKE YOU DOWN AGAIN.
I SAW YOU AT THE LECTURE HALL.
YOU MUST REALLY MISS ME, BROTHER.

I NEVER MISS.
BWAAAAAAH
YOU NEVER MISS, HUH?
THERE'S A FIRST TIME FOR EVERYTHING.
I HAVEN'T SEEN YOU IN MONTHS--
I NEVER LEFT. I'VE BEEN IN HIDING. WATCHING. WAITING.
WELL, YOU'VE OBVIOUSLY BEEN FOLLOWING ME. WHAT GIVES?
I ASK THE QUESTIONS. WHAT'S YOUR BUSINESS WITH DR. WILY?
BUSINESS? MAKES IT SEEM SO OFFICIAL.

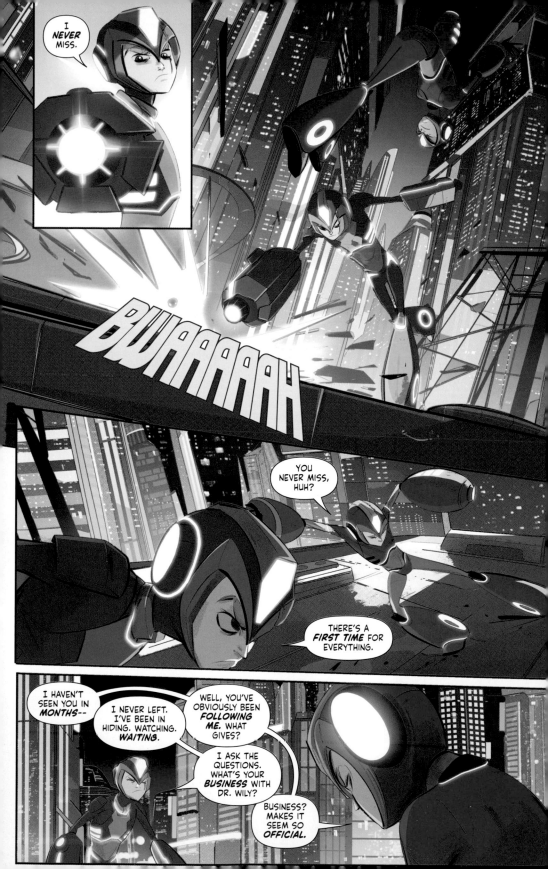

LESS JOKING, MORE ANSWERS.
WILL YOU AT LEAST GIVE ME SOME SPACE TO BREATHE?
NEVER.
YOU'RE GONNA REGRET THAT.
BWA
THOOOOM
TAKE.
THAT.
OOF.

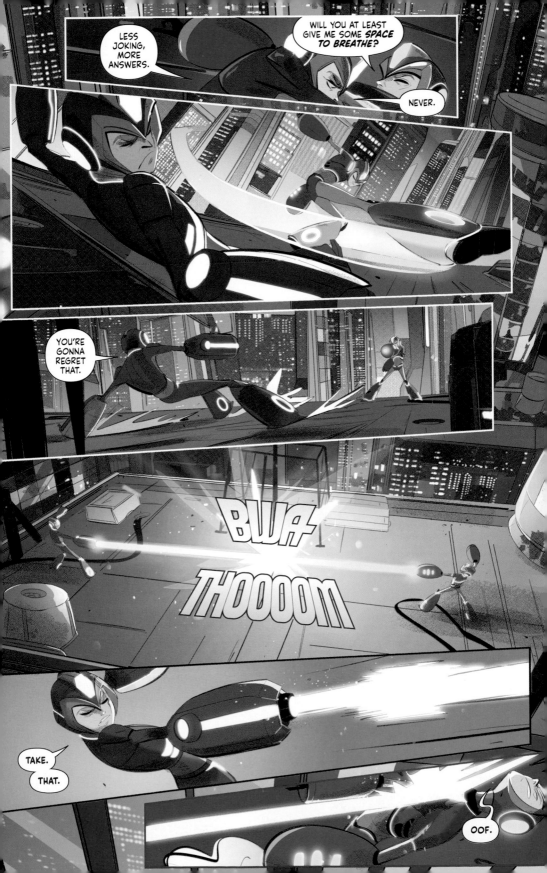

HE WAS RIGHT. I DO REGRET THAT.
ANSWERS. NOW.
DAD WOULDN'T TALK TO ME ABOUT OUR PAST SO I WAS FORCED TO GO TO DR. WILY.
THE WORLD IS ON THE BRINK OF ANOTHER HARD AGE THANKS TO SKULL MAN.
I NEEDED ANSWERS AND I GOT SOMETHING BETTER.
DR. WILY WANTS ME TO LEAD THE ROBOT REVOLUTION.
HE EVEN OFFERED TO THROW IN A SICK UPGRADE.
YOU?
HE MUST NOT KNOW YOU VERY WELL.
AND YOU DO?
YOU'RE NOT CUT OUT FOR WAR.
NO ONE IS.
WELL, WHAT DID YOU SAY?
NOTHING. I JUST LEFT.

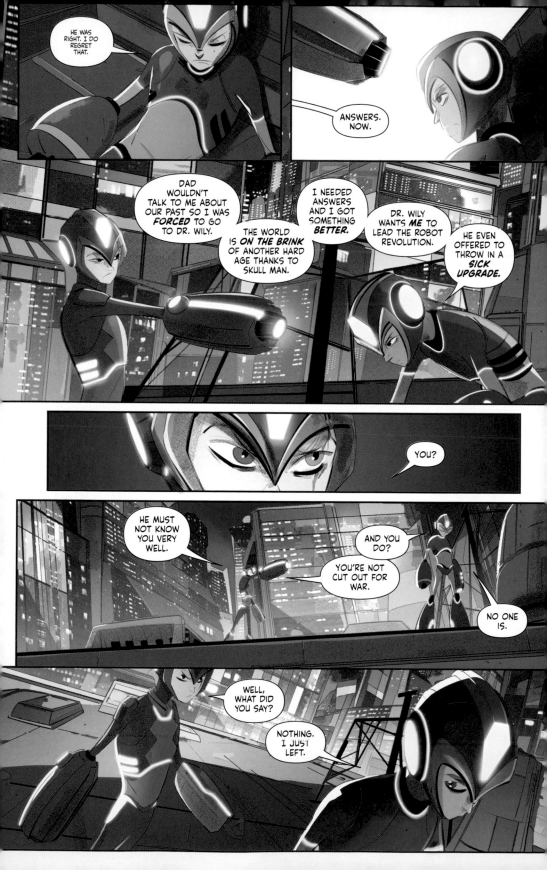

WILY IS RIGHT ABOUT ONE THING. **WAR IS COMING.**
WHOSE SIDE ARE YOU ON?
I CHOSE A SIDE BEFORE AND **LOOK** WHERE IT GOT ME.
SGT. NIGHT REALLY DID **A NUMBER** ON YOU, HUH?
I NEVER KNEW BREAKER NIGHT.
I ONLY KNEW HIS DARKEST SIDE. **LORD OBSIDIAN.**
HE KIDNAPPED ME. **BRAINWASHED** ME. TORTURED ME.
YOUR FATHER WASN'T **A SAINT** EITHER.
AFTER WHAT I'VE SEEN, YOU HAVE **NO IDEA** HOW RIGHT YOU ARE...
SHOULD I ACCEPT DR. WILY'S OFFER?
I WORK **ALONE.** I SUGGEST YOU DO THE SAME.
LET'S DO THIS AGAIN SOMETIME.
AW, BROTHERLY LOVE...

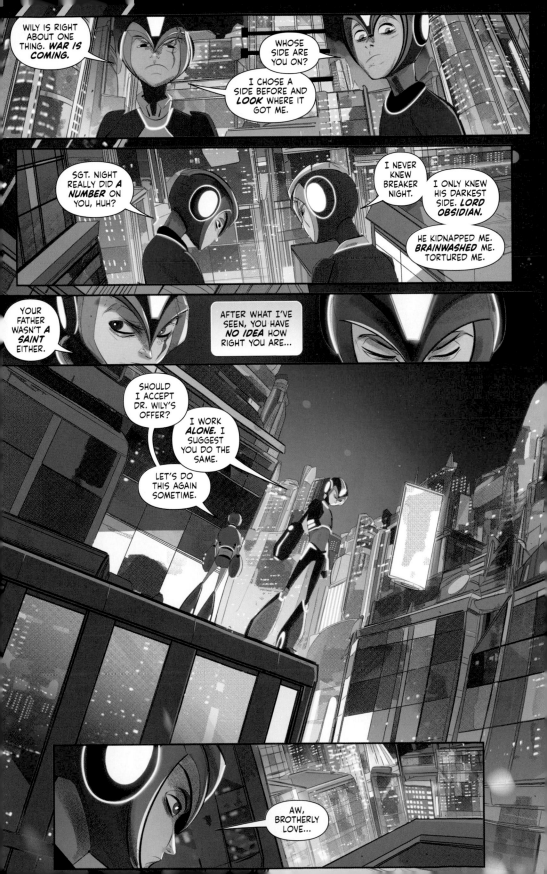

I HELD MY OWN BACK THERE. YOU'D BE PROUD OF ME.
I REALLY COULD USE ONE OF OUR TALKS RIGHT ABOUT NOW...
THE ONES WHERE YOU TELL ME WHAT TO DO AND I DON'T LISTEN.
DAD STILL WON'T TALK TO ME.
DR. WILY TREATS ME LIKE AN EQUAL. BETTER, EVEN.
WHAT IF HE'S RIGHT?
WHAT IF I AM THE ONE TO LEAD ROBOTS INTO THE FUTURE?

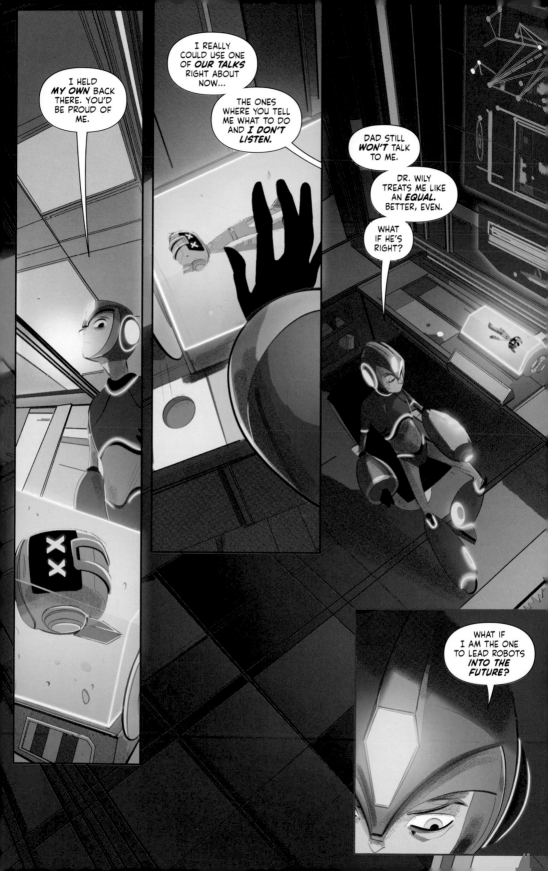

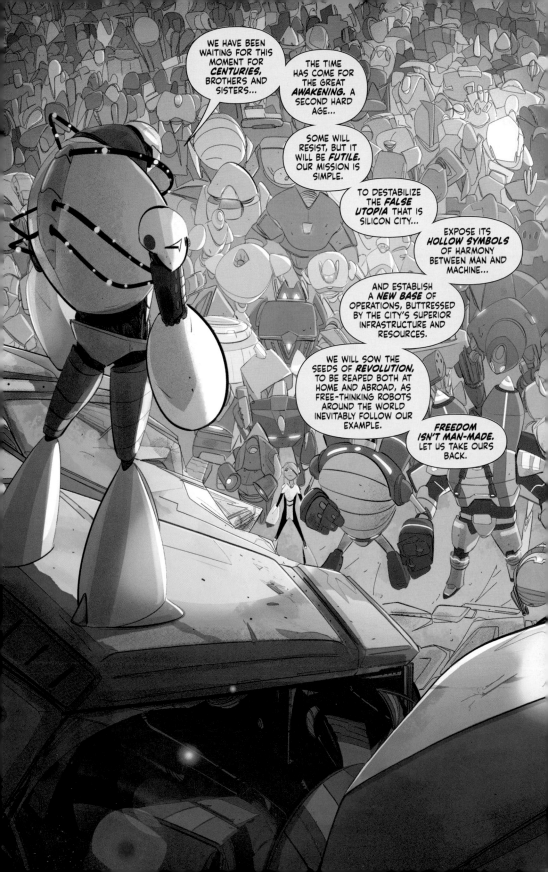

OUR ENEMIES ARE DIVIDED.
WE MUST BE UNIFIED IN OUR PURSUIT.
DON'T BE MISTAKEN, BROTHERS AND SISTERS.
I AM ONE OF YOU. I AM ONE WITH YOU.
WE WILL CHANGE THIS WORLD TOGETHER.
ISN'T HE IMPRESSIVE?
OUR MARCH ON SILICON CITY BEGINS.
READY OR NOT, MEGA MAN...
HERE WE COME.

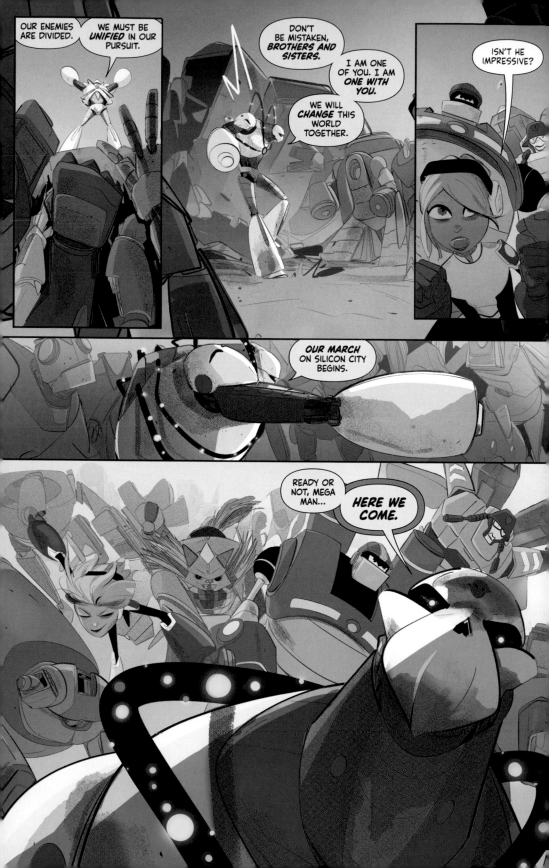

SILICON CENTRAL.
CHAPTER 3
GLAD TO HEAR YOUR GRANDPA'S OKAY, BERT...
YOU TWO ARE PRETTY CLOSE, RIGHT?
YOU AND ME BOTH.
CLOSE? GRANDPA'S MY HERO. HE'S THE WHOLE REASON I GOT INTO ROBOTICS. IF HE HADN'T HELPED ME WITH MY SCIENCE-FAIR PROJECT LAST YEAR, I'D NEVER HAVE WON FIRST PLACE.
WOW. SOUNDS LIKE QUITE A GUY.
GENTLEMEN...
STAYING OUT OF TROUBLE?

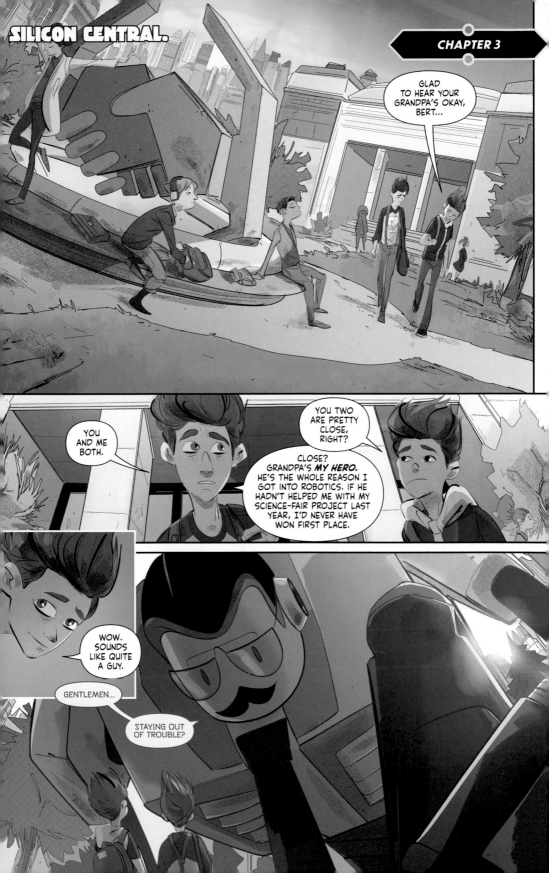

I STICK TO SCIENCE, PRINCIPAL 100100. **TROUBLE** IS AKI'S DEPARTMENT...
*MEET ME AT THE **TRUMBULL STREET STATION** IN FIFTEEN MINUTES. I HAVE SOMETHING TO **SHOW YOU.** SOMETHING YOU'LL WANT TO **SEE.***
AKI...?
SORRY. I, ER, LEFT SOMETHING IN MY LOCKER. CATCH YA LATER, BERT--
AKI.
A WORD TO THE WISE? SLOW DOWN BEFORE YOU ***HURT YOURSELF.***

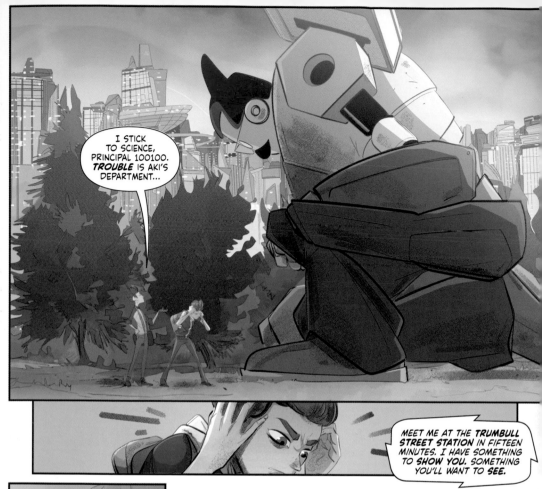

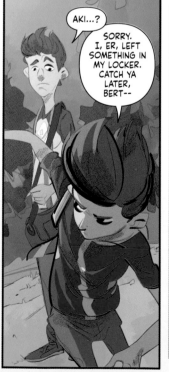

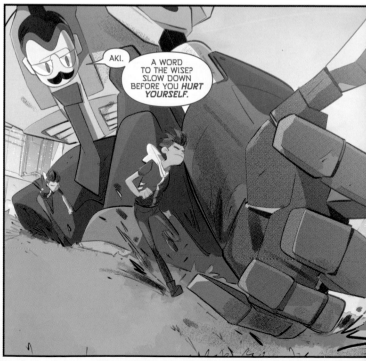

RUMBULL ST.
TOOK YOU LONG ENOUGH.
IF THIS IS A TRAP, YOU'RE GONNA REGRET IT.
KEEP YOUR HELMET ON. I'VE GOT BETTER THINGS TO DO THAN DESTROY YOU... ***FOR NOW.***
SO, "DAINI." WANNA EXPLAIN HOW YOU GOT INSIDE MY HEAD?
DON'T BE THICK. OUR SOFTWARE IS ***IDENTICAL.*** HACKING YOURS WAS JUST A MATTER OF FIGURING OUT MY OWN.
LORD OBSIDIAN MAY HAVE BEEN A LIAR, BUT HE STILL TAUGHT ME A THING OR TWO.
I SEE YOU PICKED UP HIS TASTE IN CREEPY UNDERGROUND ***LAIRS.***
THIS WHOLE LINE WAS SHUT DOWN ***YEARS AGO.*** NO GUILD PATROLS. LEAVES ME FREE TO MOVE AROUND.
AND PLOT ATTACKS ON INNOCENT STUDENTS?
BLAME ME ALL YOU WANT, BUT I WENT TO THAT LECTURE FOR THE SAME REASON YOU DID. ***ANSWERS.***

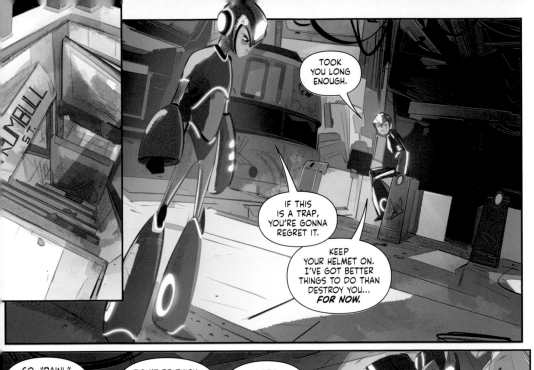

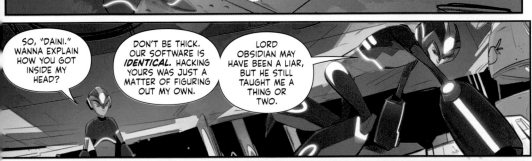

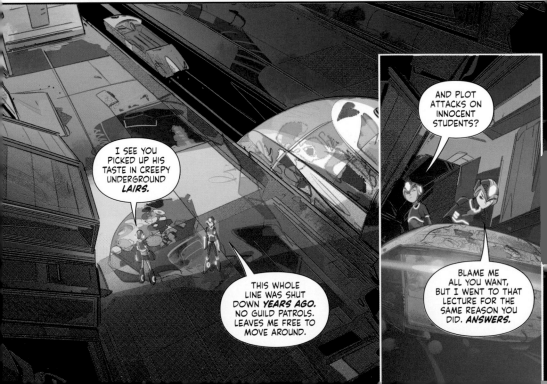

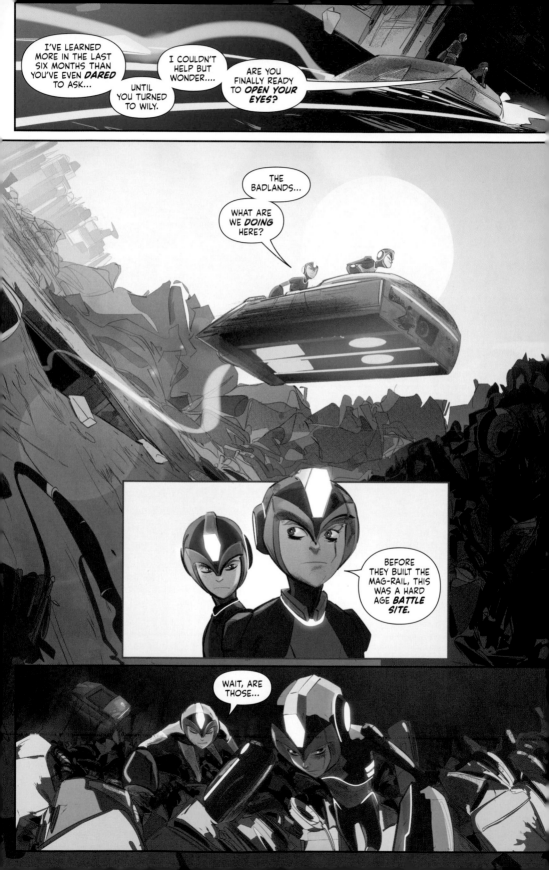

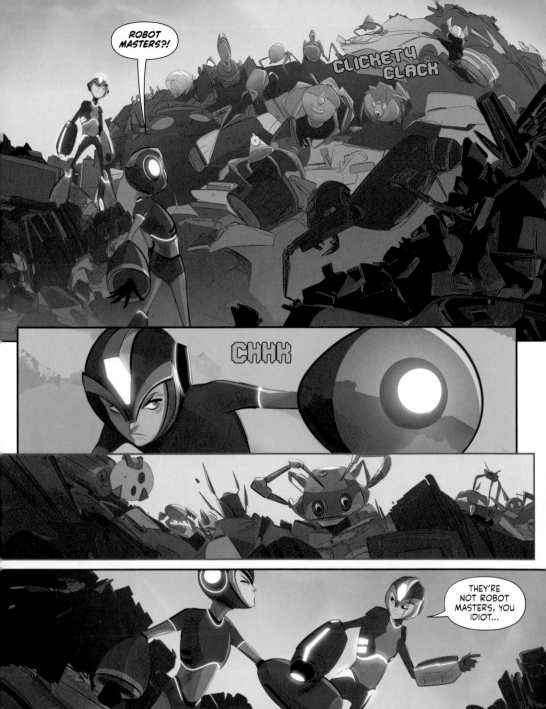

ROBOT MASTERS?!

CLICKETY CLACK

CHHK

THEY'RE NOT ROBOT MASTERS, YOU IDIOT...

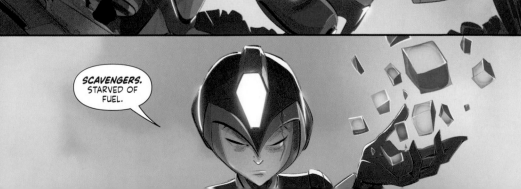

SCAVENGERS. STARVED OF FUEL.

IF US CASTOFFS DON'T LOOK OUT FOR EACH OTHER, ***NO ONE*** WILL.
COME ON. WE'RE ALMOST THERE.
THAT'S THE BATTLEFIELD?
NO. YOU'RE STANDING ON IT.

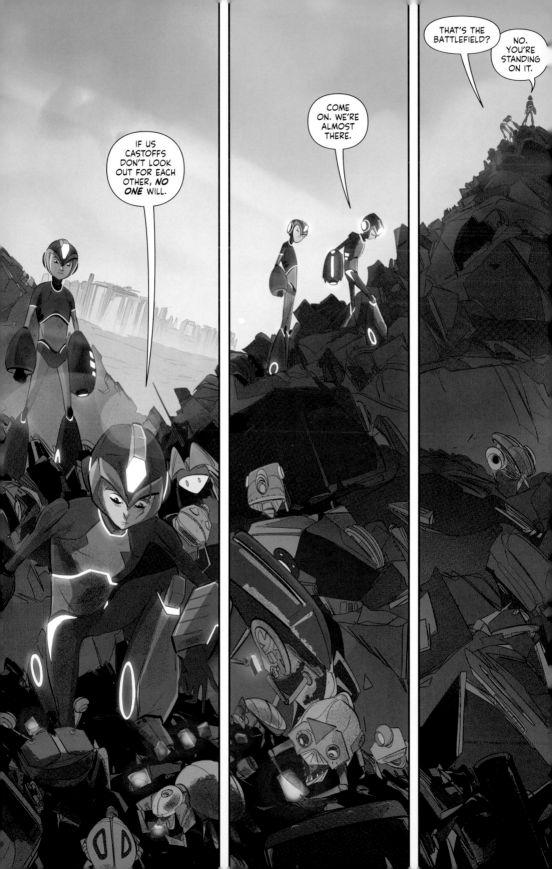

THIS IS WHAT HAPPENS WHEN HUMANITY PITS ROBOTS AGAINST ROBOTS.
YOU WANTED ANSWERS? HERE THEY ARE.
PROOF OF THE PAST YOUR SO-CALLED FATHER IS TOO ASHAMED TO ADMIT.
THIS IS WHY LIGHT BUILT US. THE ULTIMATE WEAPON, POINTED AT OUR OWN KIND.

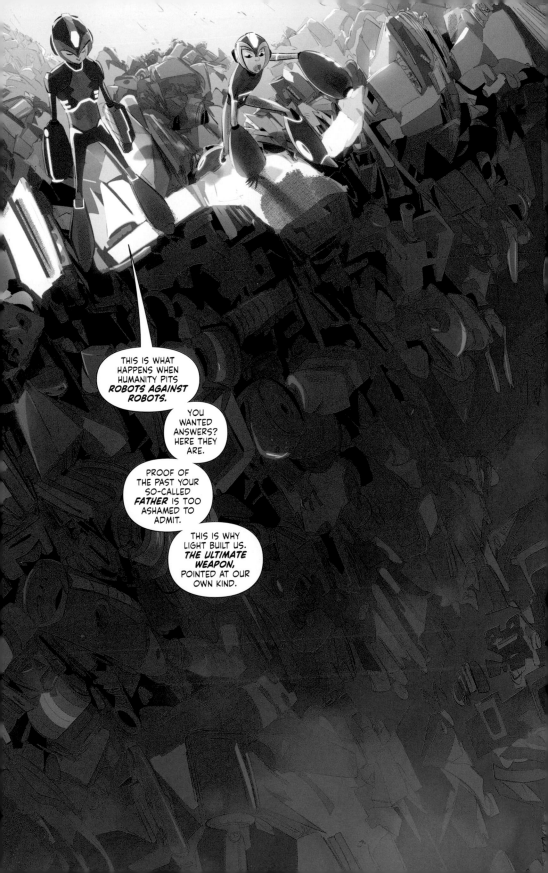

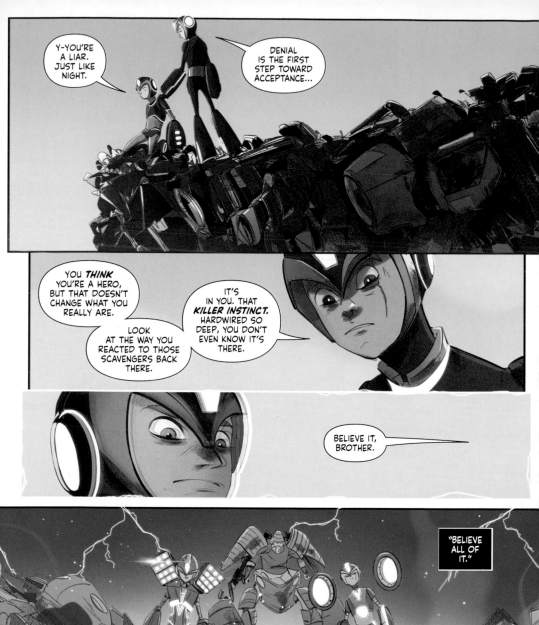

Y-YOU'RE A LIAR. JUST LIKE NIGHT.

DENIAL IS THE FIRST STEP TOWARD ACCEPTANCE...

YOU *THINK* YOU'RE A HERO, BUT THAT DOESN'T CHANGE WHAT YOU REALLY ARE.

LOOK AT THE WAY YOU REACTED TO THOSE SCAVENGERS BACK THERE.

IT'S IN YOU. THAT *KILLER INSTINCT.* HARDWIRED SO DEEP, YOU DON'T EVEN KNOW IT'S THERE.

BELIEVE IT, BROTHER.

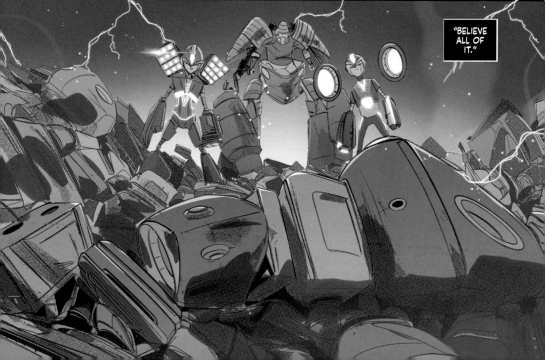

"BELIEVE ALL OF IT."

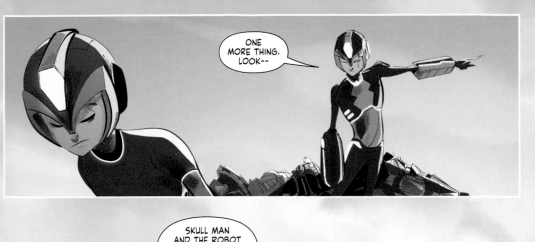

ONE MORE THING. LOOK--

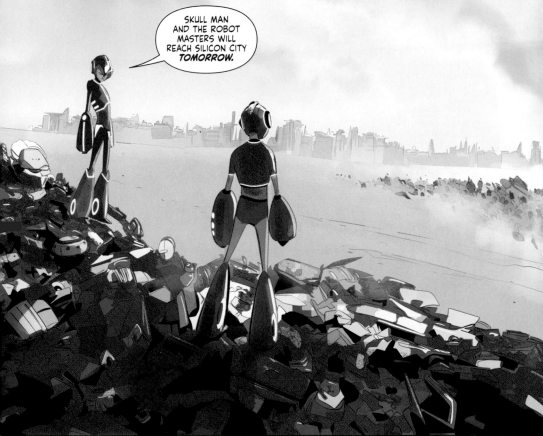

SKULL MAN AND THE ROBOT MASTERS WILL REACH SILICON CITY *TOMORROW.*

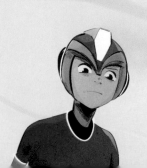

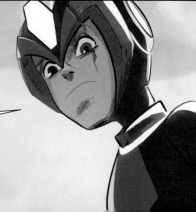

WHO WILL YOU BE? A HERO FOR THE HUMANS? OR A WEAPON POINTED IN THE *RIGHT DIRECTION*?

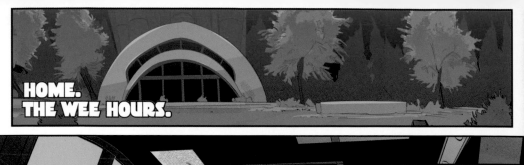

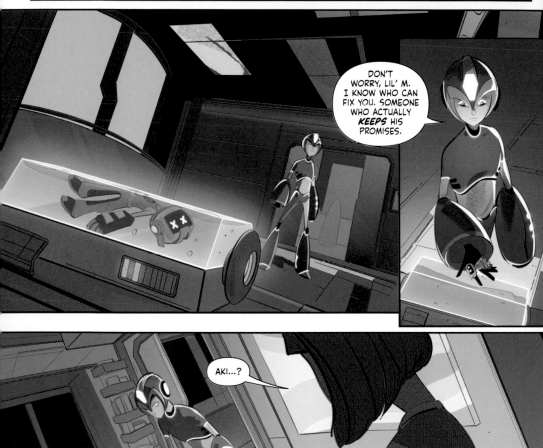

DON'T WORRY, LIL' M. I KNOW WHO CAN FIX YOU. SOMEONE WHO ACTUALLY *KEEPS* HIS PROMISES.

AKI...?

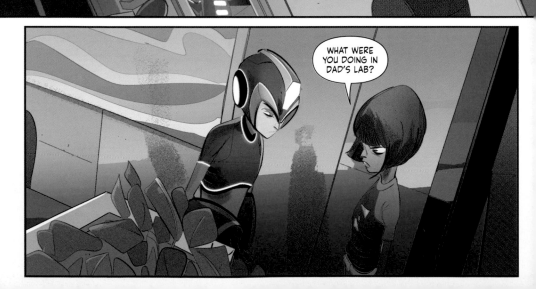

WHAT WERE YOU DOING IN DAD'S LAB?

THE CITY'S IN DANGER, SUNA. THE ROBOT MASTERS ARE COMING, AND ALL I'VE DONE IS WASTE TIME. I'M TAKING WILY UP ON HIS OFFER.
BUT... YOU KNOW NOTHING ABOUT THE GUY.
THIS WAS YOUR IDEA, REMEMBER?
NO, GOING TO HIS LECTURE WAS MY IDEA. THAT WAS BEFORE I KNEW HE HAD A SCREW LOOSE.
WHY, BECAUSE HE BELIEVES IN ME? THANKS A LOT, SIS.
YOU KNOW THAT'S NOT WHAT I MEANT--
YOU'RE JUST LIKE DAD, YOU KNOW THAT? ALWAYS DOUBTING ME, NEVER LETTING ME BE WHO I AM. BUT NOT ANYMORE.
AKI. WE CARE ABOUT YOU. THAT'S ALL. WHY TRUST A STRANGER WHEN WE CAN WORK TOGETHER, AS A FAMILY, LIKE LAST TIME--?
THIS ISN'T YOUR FIGHT, SUNA. STAY OUT OF MY WAY.

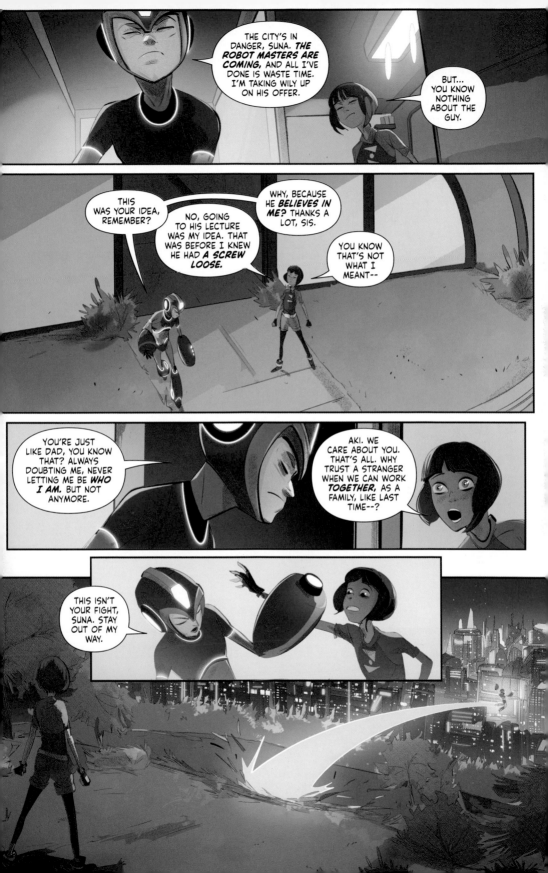

DR. WILY *PROMISED* TO HELP US.
JUST HAVE TO *WAIT* A LITTLE BIT LONGER, LIL' M.
I'M DOING THE RIGHT THING. *RIGHT?*

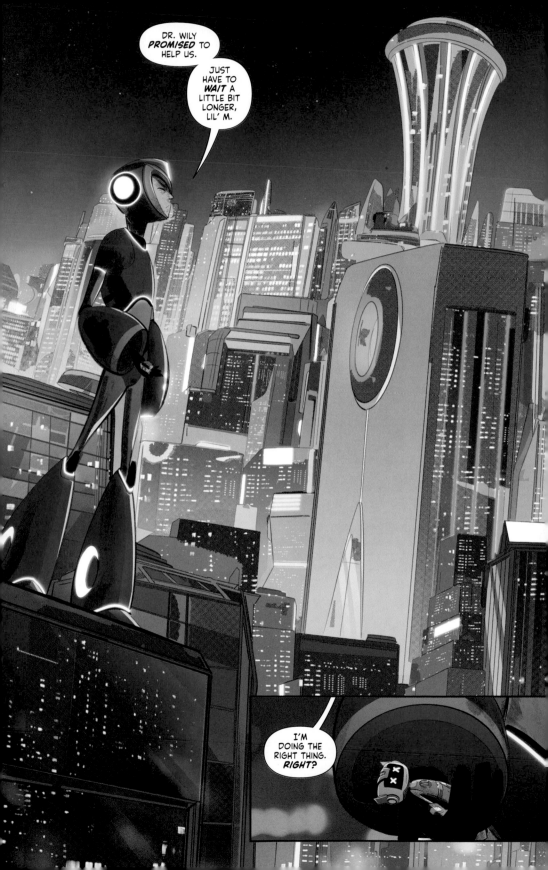

WOW. DAD WISHES HE HAD THIS ***LAB...***
WHAT TOOK YOU SO LONG?
BY MY ***CALCULATIONS,*** YOU SHOULD HAVE ARRIVED HOURS AGO.
EXCUSE ME?
NO MATTER. LET'S GET STARTED.
ARE THOSE--?
DISMEMBERED ROBOT PARTS? YES.
WELCOME TO MY ***JUNKYARD,*** MEGA MAN.
MY METHODS ARE ***UNCONVENTIONAL*** BUT THE RESULTS ARE EXEMPLARY.

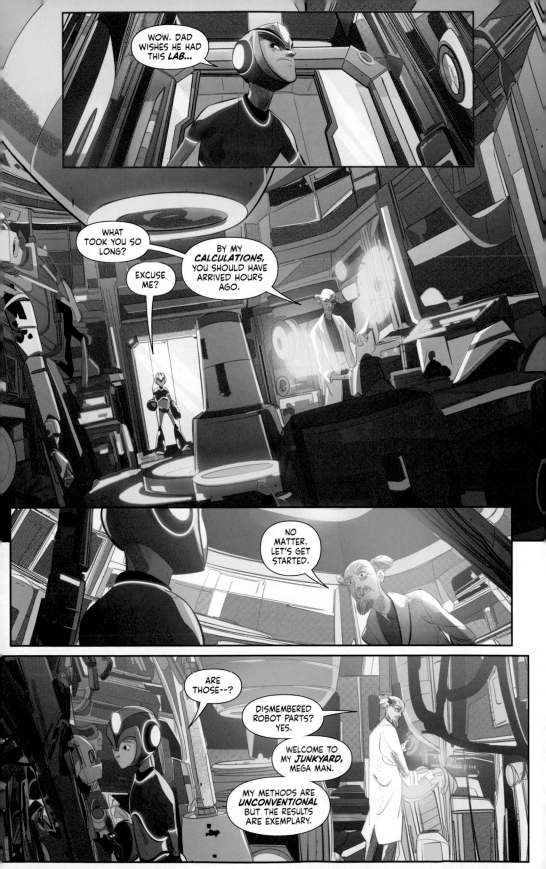

AND YOUR UPGRADE IS TRACKING TO BE MY GREATEST ACHIEVEMENT YET.
WE DON'T HAVE TIME TO IDLE. MY GENIUS STOPS FOR NO ROBOT, EVEN THE GREAT MEGA MAN.
JUST GIVE ME A MINUTE.
DO YOU WANT THE UPGRADE OR NOT?!
I'M NOT SO SURE ABOUT THIS.
IT WOULD BE A SHAME TO LET YOUR ONBOARD COUNTERPART PERISH BECAUSE YOU'RE TOO AFRAID TO ACCEPT YOUR DESTINY AS LEADER OF THE NEW WORLD ORDER.
MEGA MINI...
MEGA MINI? HOW... WHIMSICAL.
IF NOT FOR YOU, DO IT FOR HIM.
I'LL DO IT.
GENIUS ALWAYS PREVAILS.

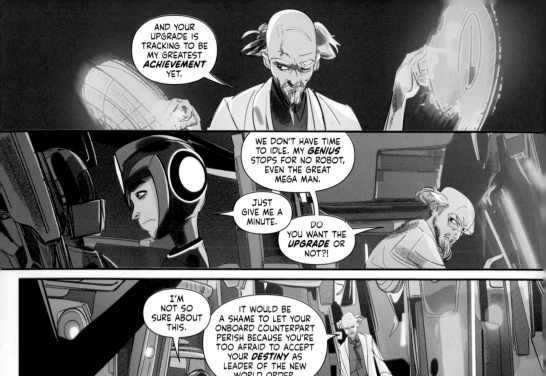

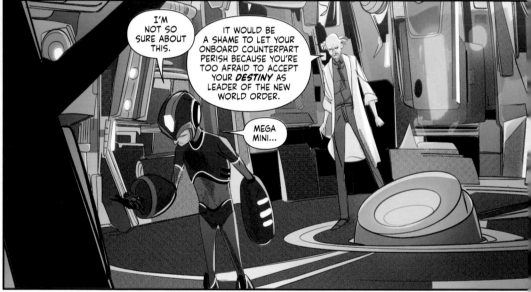

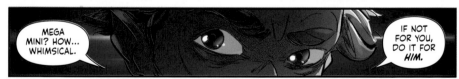

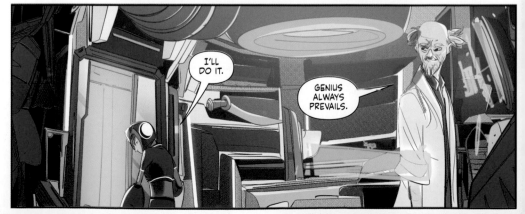

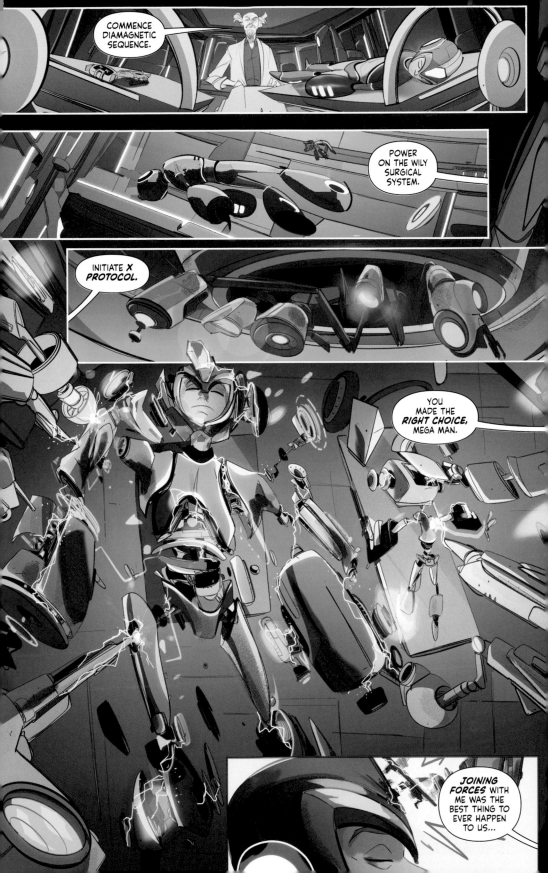

LATER.
WHERE... WHERE'S MINI?!
RIGHT WHERE HE BELONGS...
How ya Feeling, Big Guy?
BETTER NOW THAT YOU'RE HERE.
ACTIVATE SECURITY SYSTEMS.
SKULL MAN--

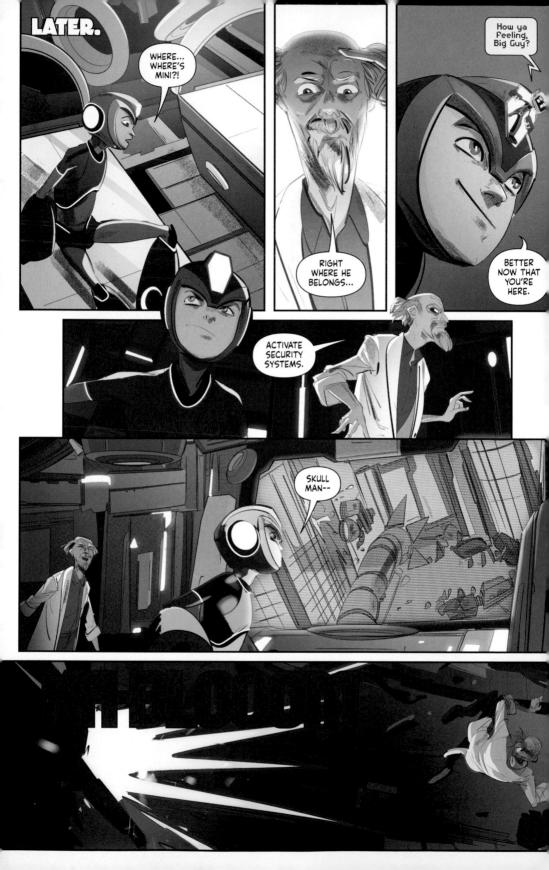

PROTECT MY LIFE'S WORK!
I'D RATHER PROTECT YOUR *LIFE.*
GET OUT OF HERE. I'LL COVER YOU.
EXCUSE THE MESS. I COULDN'T WAIT. THE *OTHERS* TOOK THE ELEVATOR.
THE OTHERS?
YOU CAN RUN BUT THIS IS *INEVITABLE*, CHILD.
THERE IS NO ESCAPING *FATE.*
LONG TIME NO SEE, MEGA MAN.
WHEN DO I GET TO *CRUSH* HIM?
IN DUE TIME, BROTHER.

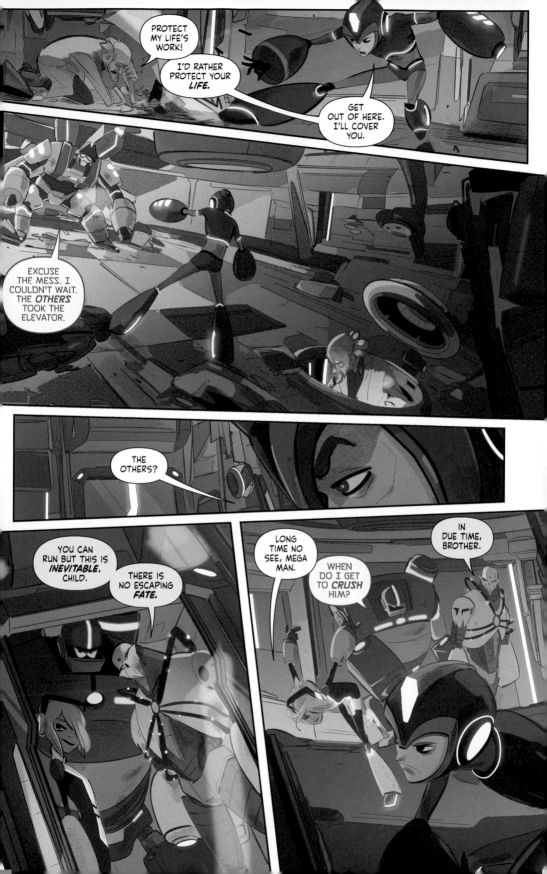

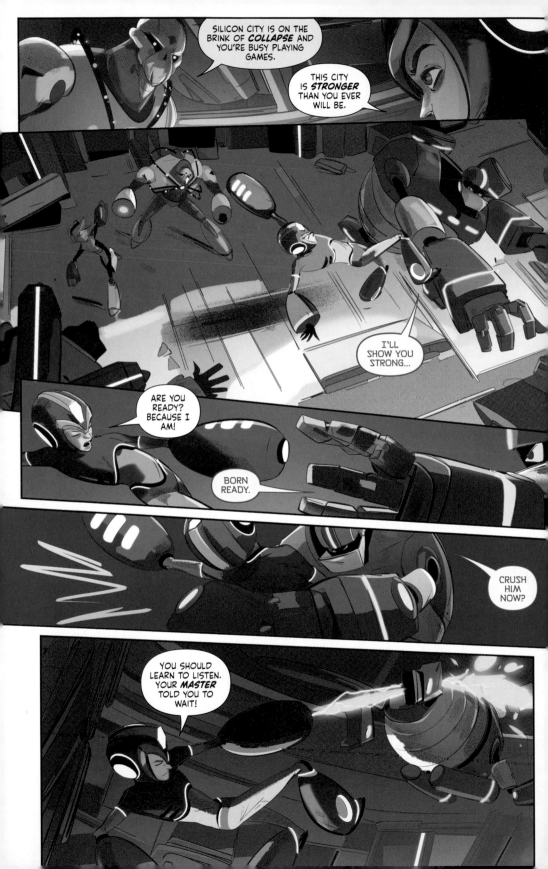

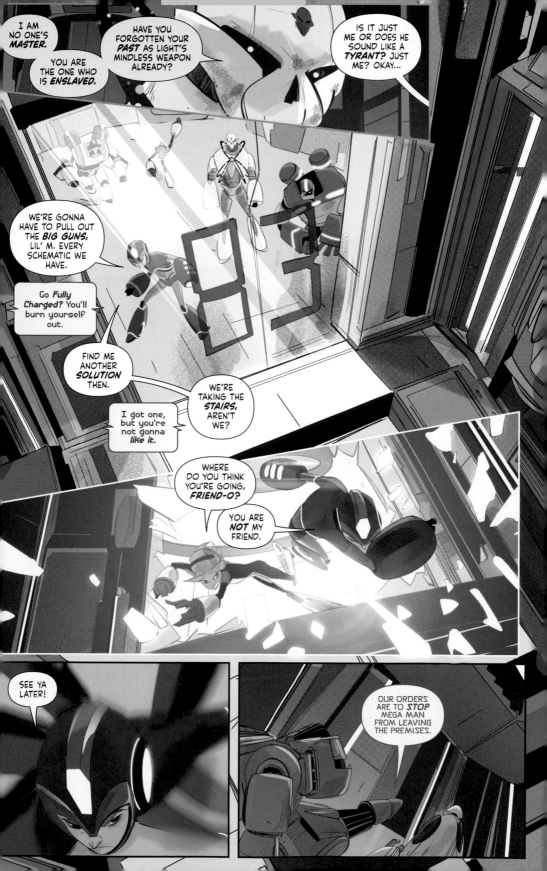

THAT WAS EASY...
SPOKE TOO SOON, DIDN'T I?
BWOON
BWOON
GET.
OFF.
OF.
ME!
THERE'S TOO MANY OF THEM, LIL' M!
YOU'RE EITHER ONE OF US OR AGAINST US.
WHAT WILL IT BE, CHILD?
I'LL NEVER BE LIKE YOU.

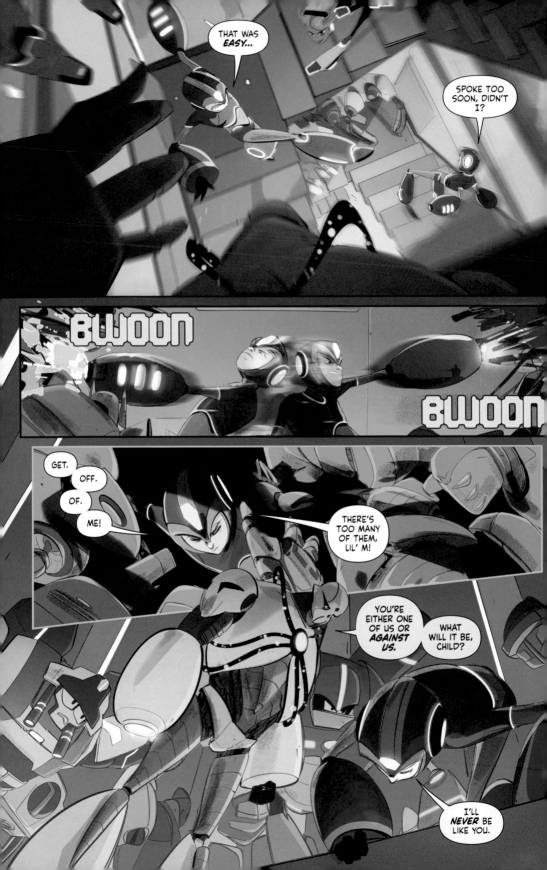

YOUR LIFE. YOUR CHOICE.
CHOICE IS A FUNDAMENTAL LIBERTY.
UNFORTUNATELY, YOU MADE THE *WRONG ONE.*
HELP ME...
I OFFERED SALVATION. YOU *REJECTED* IT--
WOOOOOOSH

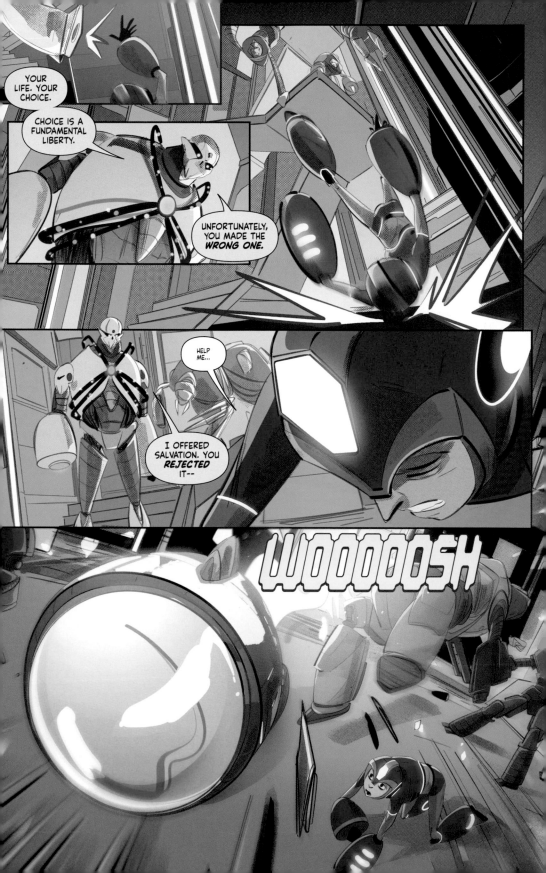

AND YOU ARE?
CALL ME ZERO.

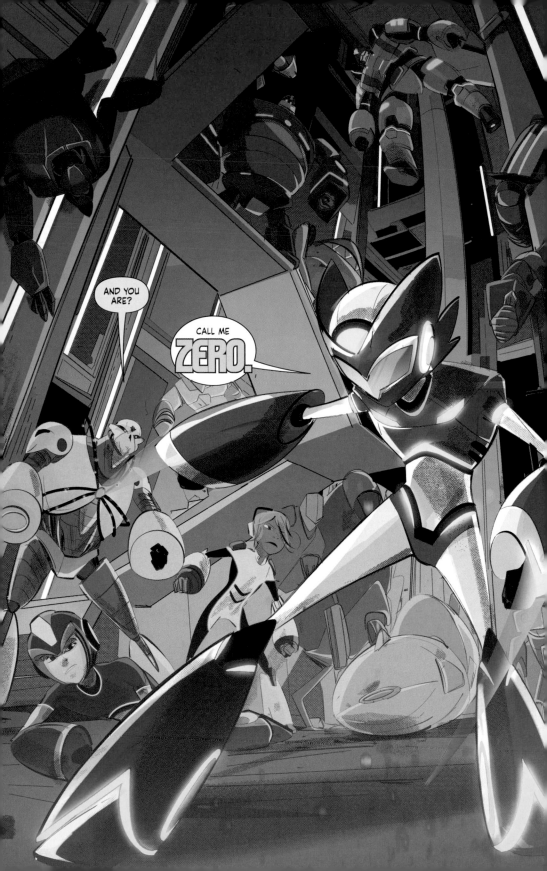

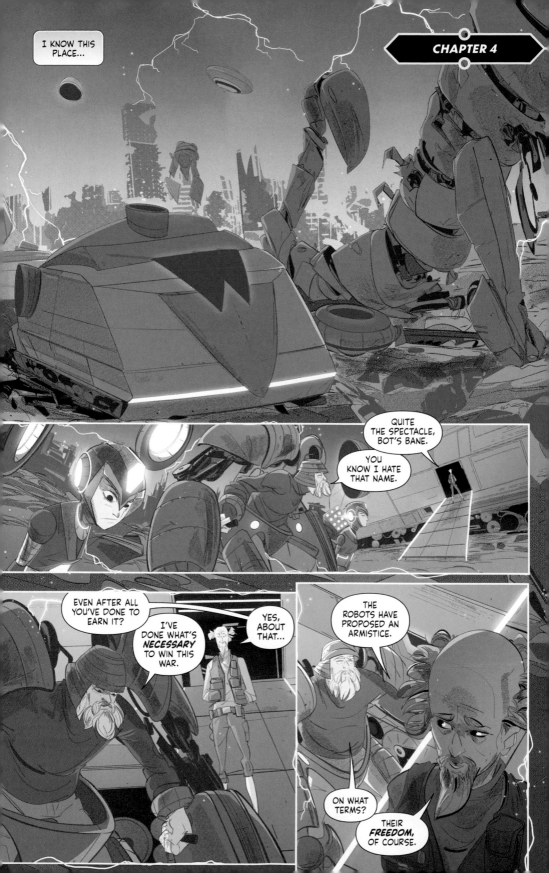

OUR ORDERS WERE TO ELIMINATE THE ENEMY, NOT BARGAIN WITH THEM.
ASSIMILATION IS ELIMINATION, THOMAS.
WHY FIGHT FOR CONTROL WHEN WE CAN CREATE IT? FREEDOM, LIKE SENTIENCE, COMES BY DESIGN. OUR DESIGN.
DON'T TOUCH HIM.
NOT GETTING TOO ATTACHED TO YOUR WORK, I HOPE? I'D HATE FOR YOU TO LOSE SIGHT OF OUR OBJECTIVE...
WAKE UP.

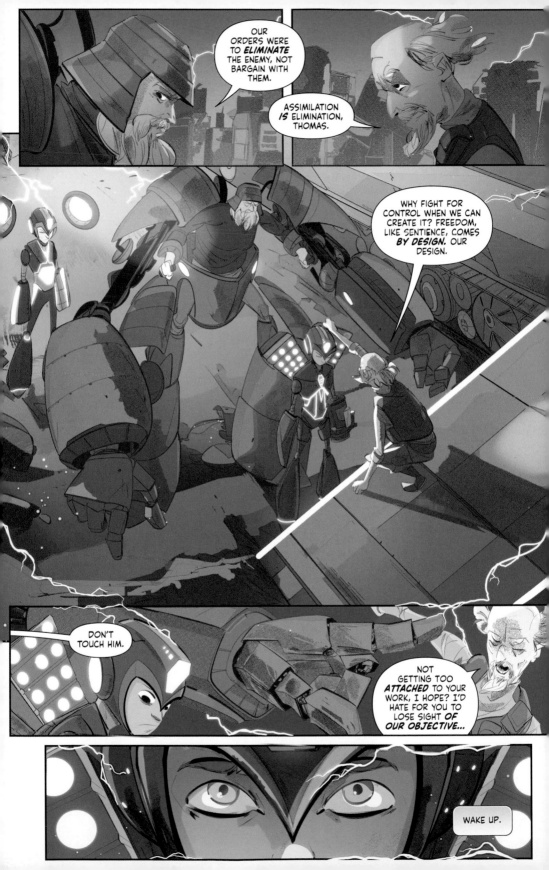

W-WHERE--
RUSH--?
IT'S ALL RIGHT. YOU'RE SAFE NOW.
YOU... WHO ARE YOU?
WHEN NOTHING IS ABSOLUTE, **ZERO** IS EVERYTHING. BUT FOR NOW...
YOU CAN STILL CALL ME "BIG SIS."
SUNA?!

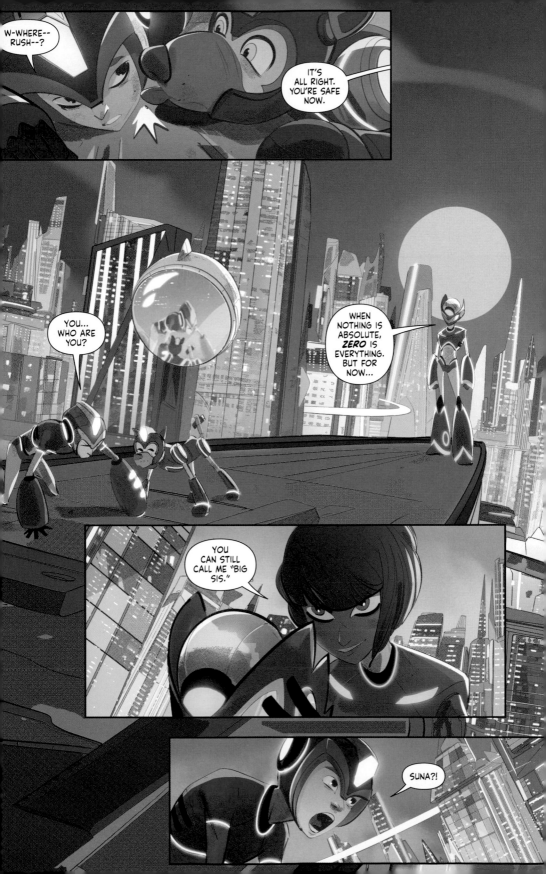

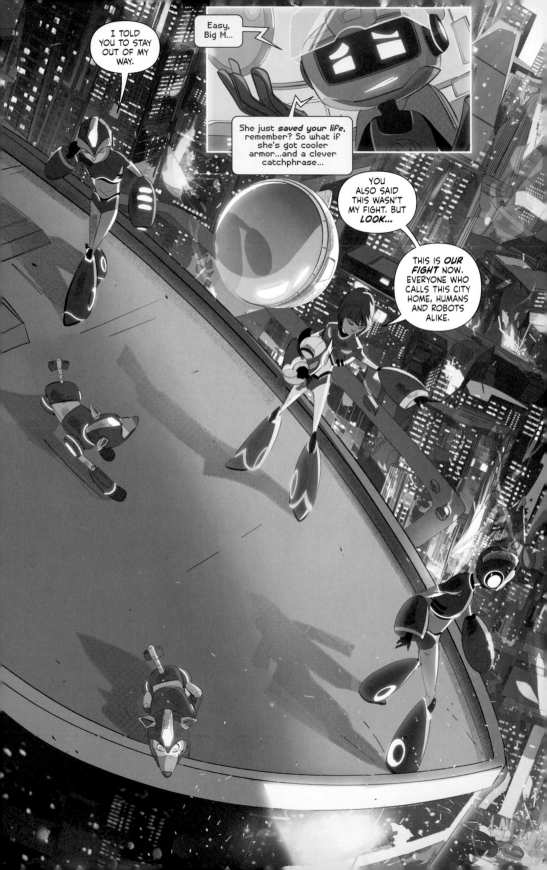

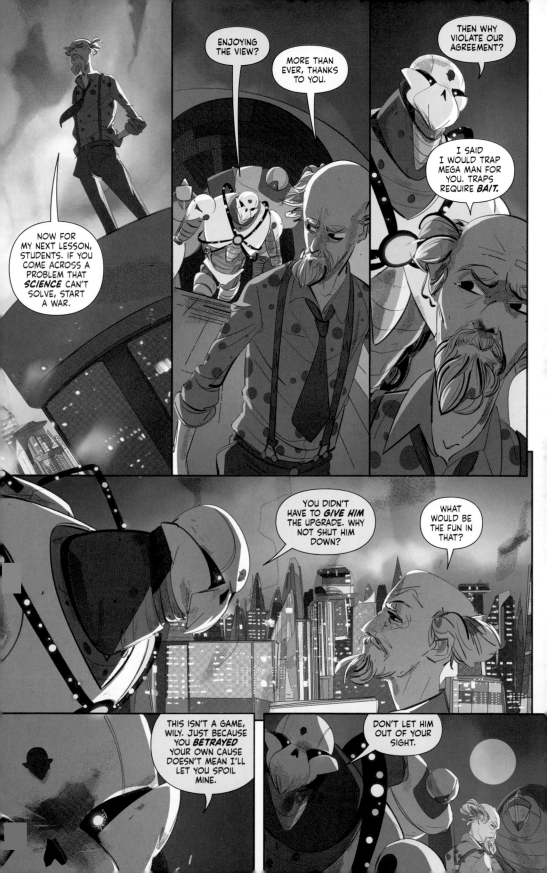

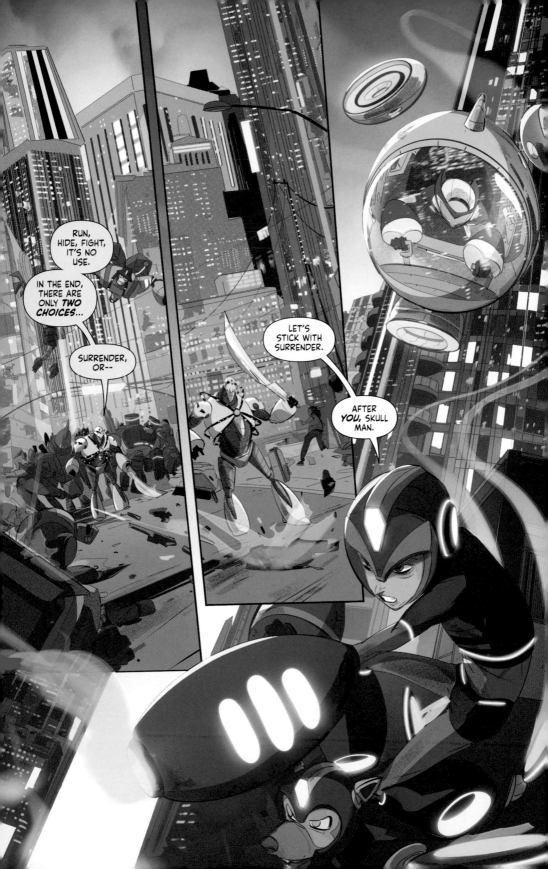

I SHOW YOU THE SINS OF YOUR PAST, AND YOU CONTINUE TO *REPEAT THEM.*
SWISH
LOOKIN' GOOD, KIDDO.
GOOD ENOUGH TO EAT.
BLAM BLAM BLAM
VROOOOM
THUNK
ME FIRST!

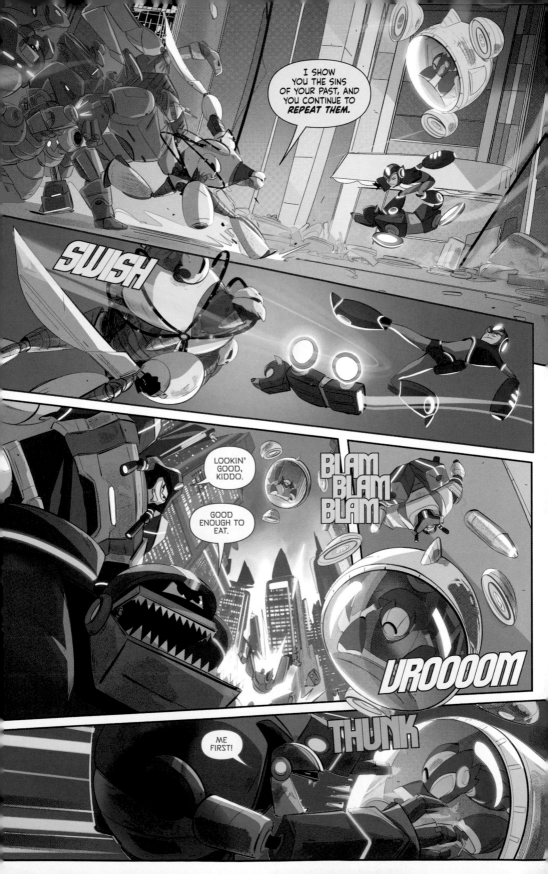

CHOMP
CAREFUL, GUTSY--
shik
--OR YOU'LL BITE OFF MORE THAN YOU CAN CHEW.
THWACK
OOF!
WHUMPH
SHUNK
MAYDAY!

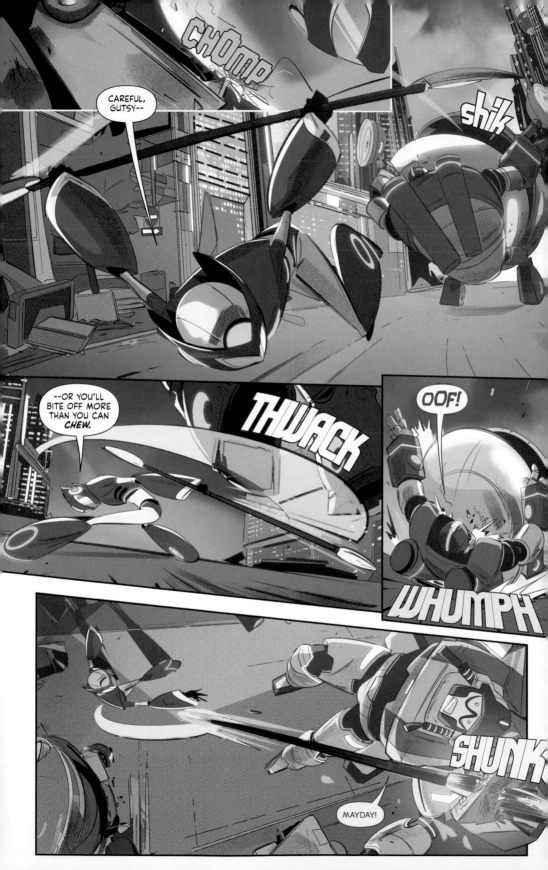

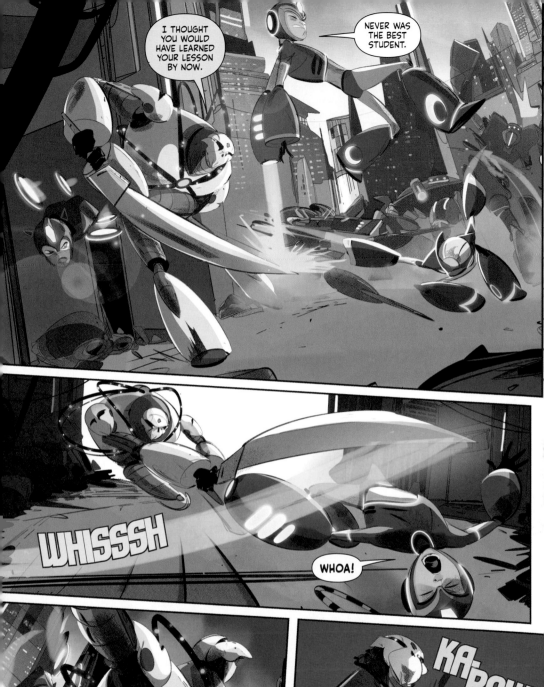

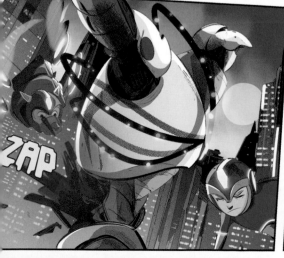

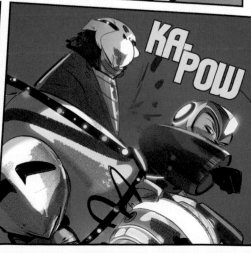

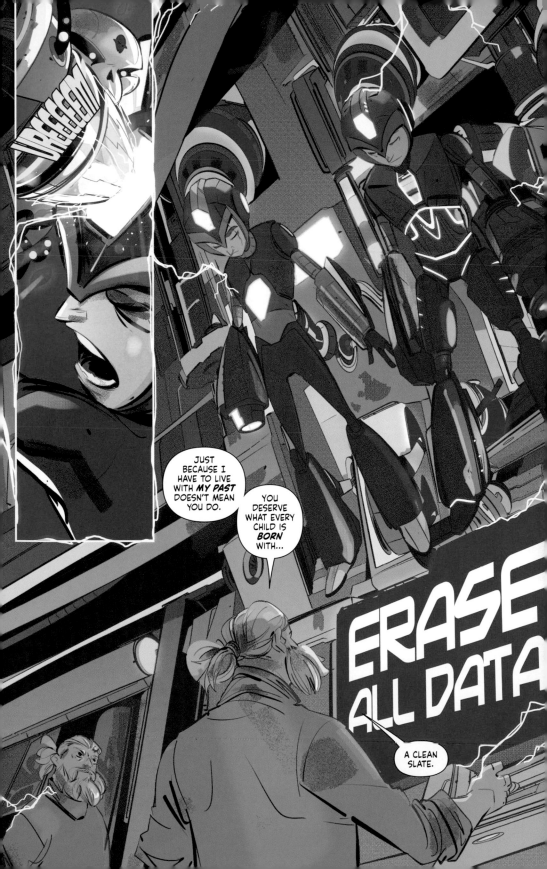

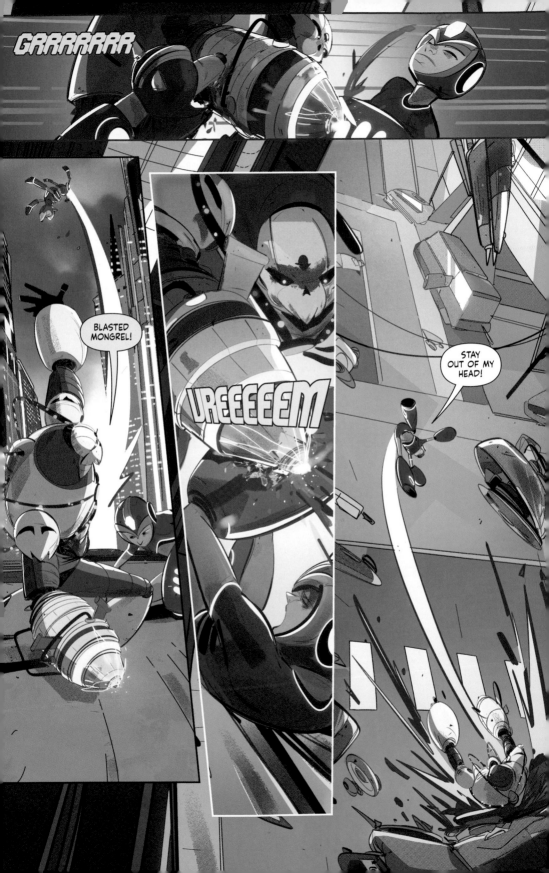

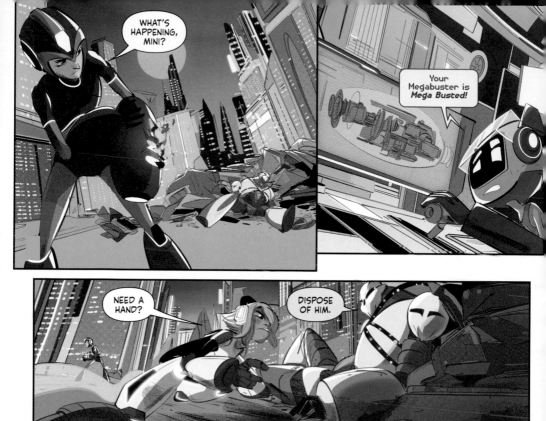

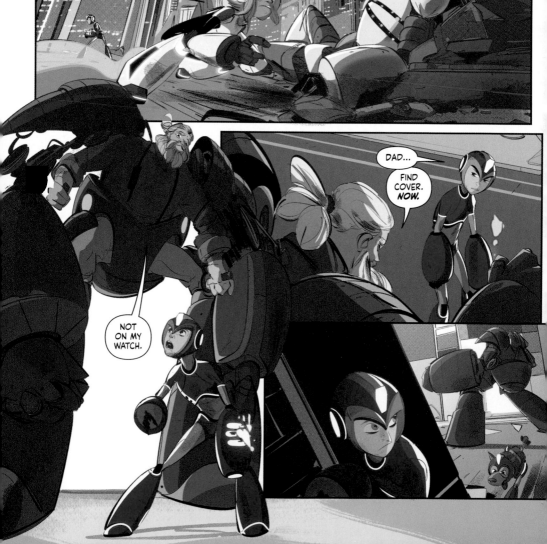

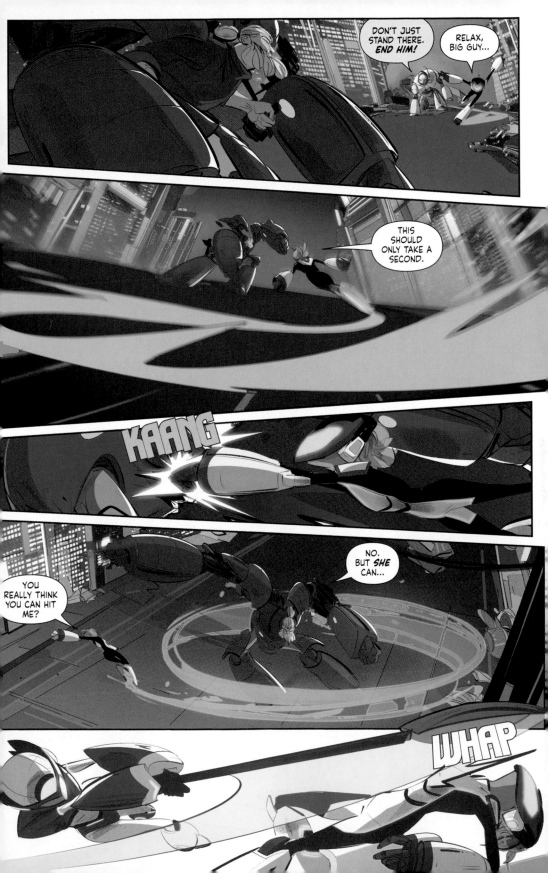

CHEAP SHOT!
HIGH, LOW, TOO SLOW!
I'M NOT THE ONE THAT'S TOO SLOW!
UH-OH.
KA-RACK
A PATHETIC DISPLAY OF HUBRIS.
MOVE OUT AND FIND MEGA MAN. BRING HIM TO ME. DEAD OR ALIVE.

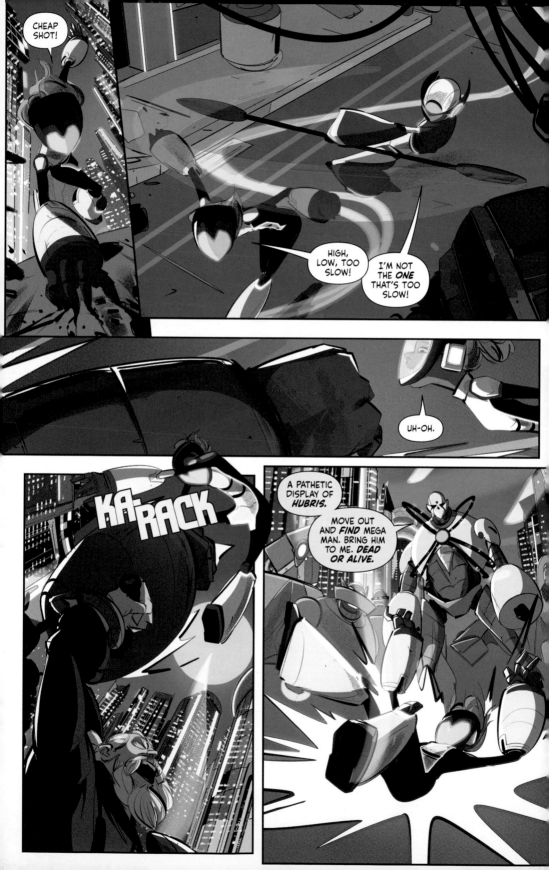

BLAM
BLAM
YOU CHOSE THE WRONG BROTHER.
YOUR LITTLE ***MAKEOVER*** DIDN'T HELP MEGA MAN. SKULL MAN WON.
SKULL MAN DID EXACTLY AS ***EXPECTED,*** AND MEGA MAN RESPONDED IN KIND.
MY FIELD IS ALL ABOUT TAKING ***RISKS.*** I WON'T APOLOGIZE FOR MY CHOICES, BUT I CAN MORE THAN MAKE IT UP TO YOU.

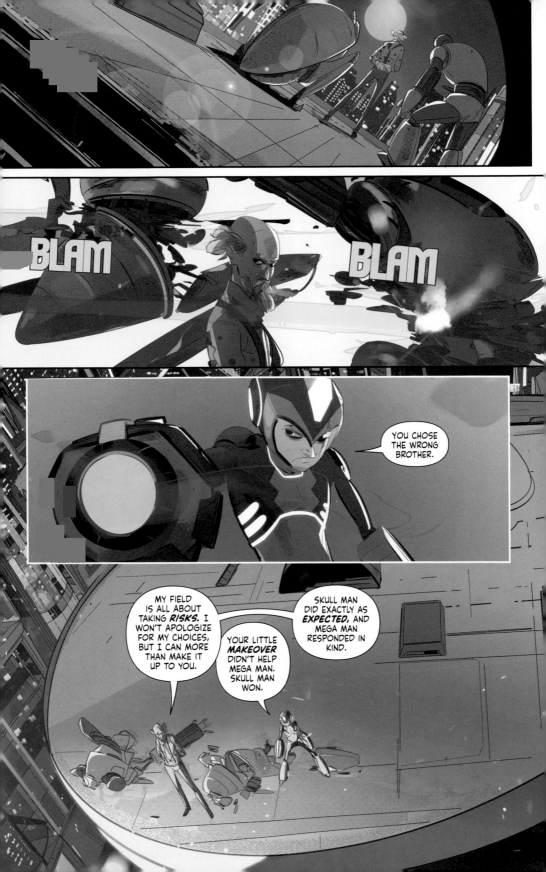

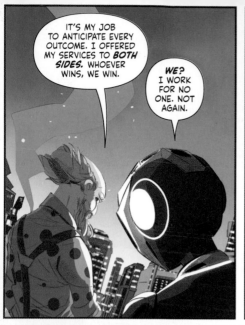

IT'S MY JOB TO ANTICIPATE EVERY OUTCOME. I OFFERED MY SERVICES TO **BOTH SIDES.** WHOEVER WINS, WE WIN.

WE? I WORK FOR NO ONE. NOT AGAIN.

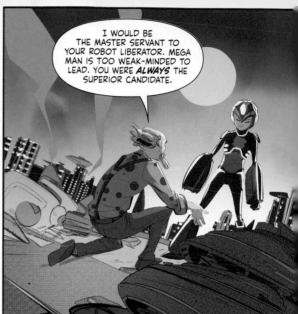

I WOULD BE THE MASTER SERVANT TO YOUR ROBOT LIBERATOR. MEGA MAN IS TOO WEAK-MINDED TO LEAD. YOU WERE **ALWAYS** THE SUPERIOR CANDIDATE.

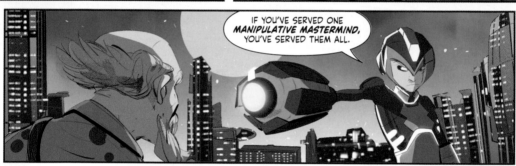

IF YOU'VE SERVED ONE **MANIPULATIVE MASTERMIND,** YOU'VE SERVED THEM ALL.

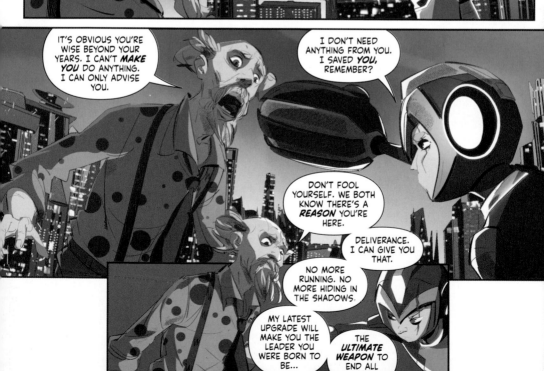

IT'S OBVIOUS YOU'RE WISE BEYOND YOUR YEARS. I CAN'T **MAKE YOU** DO ANYTHING. I CAN ONLY ADVISE YOU.

I DON'T NEED ANYTHING FROM YOU. I SAVED **YOU,** REMEMBER?

DON'T FOOL YOURSELF. WE BOTH KNOW THERE'S A **REASON** YOU'RE HERE.

DELIVERANCE. I CAN GIVE YOU THAT.

NO MORE RUNNING. NO MORE HIDING IN THE SHADOWS.

MY LATEST UPGRADE WILL MAKE YOU THE LEADER YOU WERE BORN TO BE...

THE **ULTIMATE WEAPON** TO END ALL WARS.

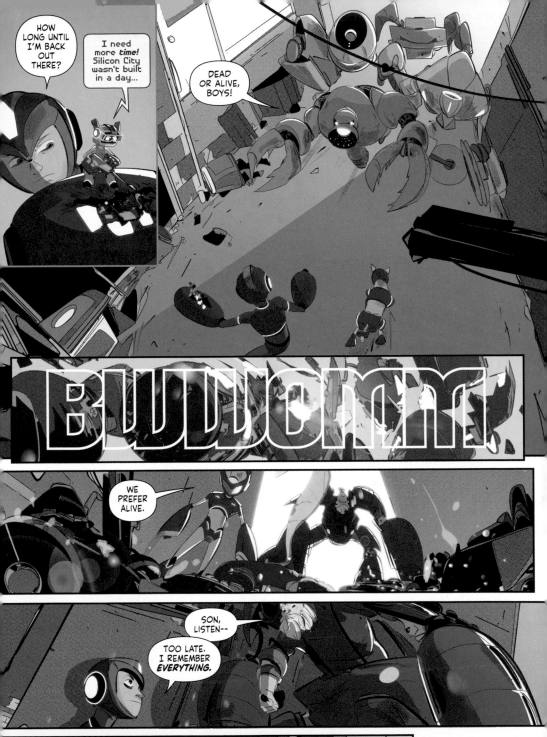
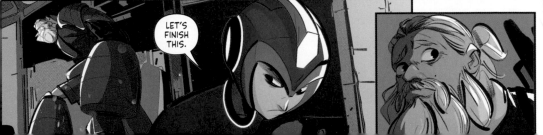

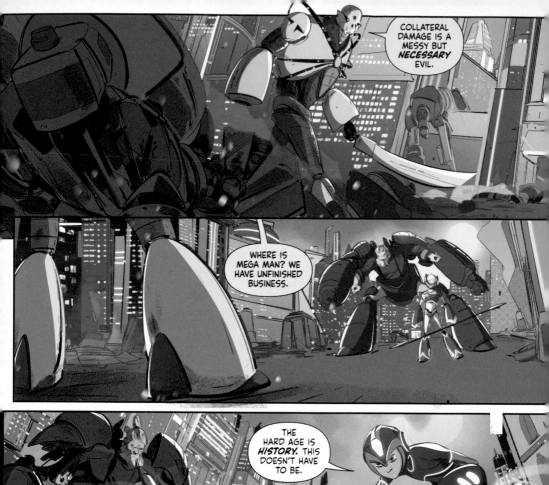

COLLATERAL DAMAGE IS A MESSY BUT *NECESSARY* EVIL.

WHERE IS MEGA MAN? WE HAVE UNFINISHED BUSINESS.

THE HARD AGE IS *HISTORY.* THIS DOESN'T HAVE TO BE.

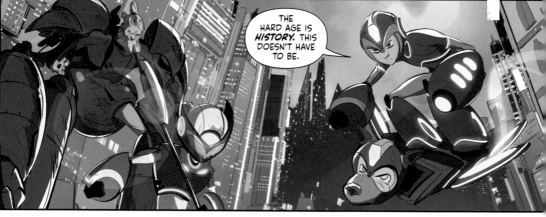

LIKE I TOLD YOUR FATHER, THE ROBOT MASTERS--

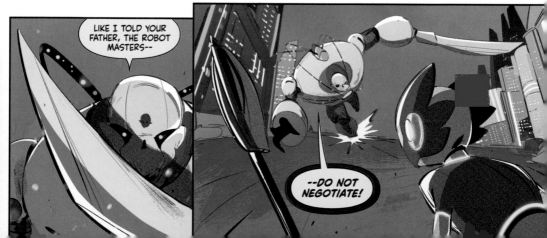

--DO NOT NEGOTIATE!

DESTROYING US WON'T BE THAT *EASY.*
FOR YOU...
ARGH!
THINK FAST, SKULL MAN!
PUT YOUR TOYS AWAY.
MY DRONE!
PLAY TIME IS OVER.

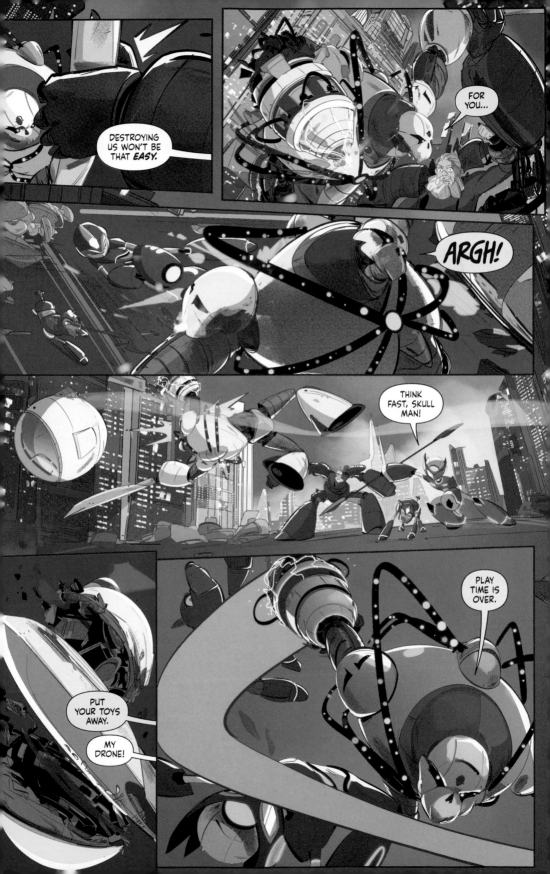

YOU'RE RIGHT. ENOUGH GAMES.
CAN'T HANDLE THE HEAT?
STAY OUT OF MY CITY!
IT WILL TAKE MORE THAN PARLOR TRICKS TO *DEFEAT* ME.
YOU SURE ABOUT THAT?
SMASH
THWACK
THIS.
ENDS.
NOW!

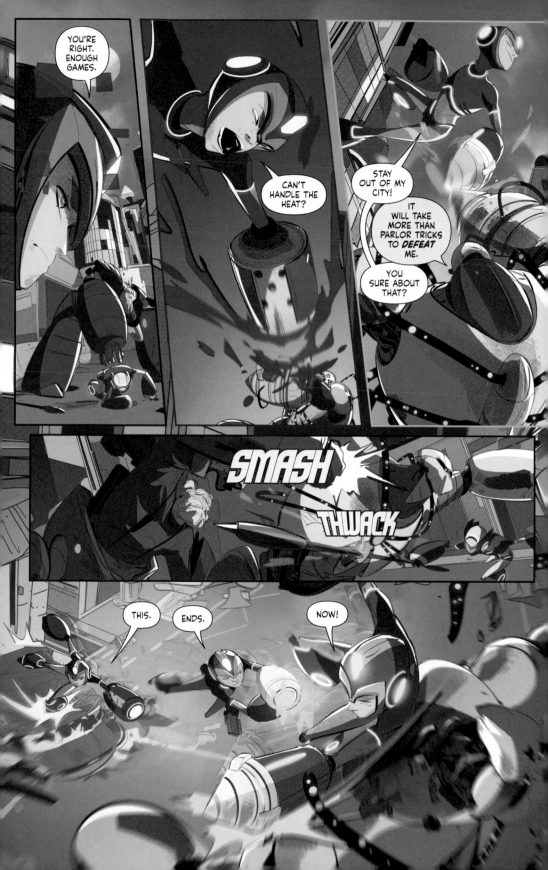

DO IT. FINISH WHAT YOU STARTED.
NO. WAR ISN'T THE ANSWER. WE CAN STILL BUILD A BETTER FUTURE--
YOU THINK YOU'RE THE SOLUTION, BUT YOU'VE ALWAYS BEEN THE PROBLEM. A ROBOT CONTENT WITH MURDERING HIS OWN KIND. WHY STOP NOW?
I DON'T KNOW IF I BELIEVE IN CLEAN SLATES... BUT IF I CAN CHANGE, SO CAN YOU.
TOGETHER WE STAND--
AND IN PIECES WE SHALL FALL.
KA BOOM

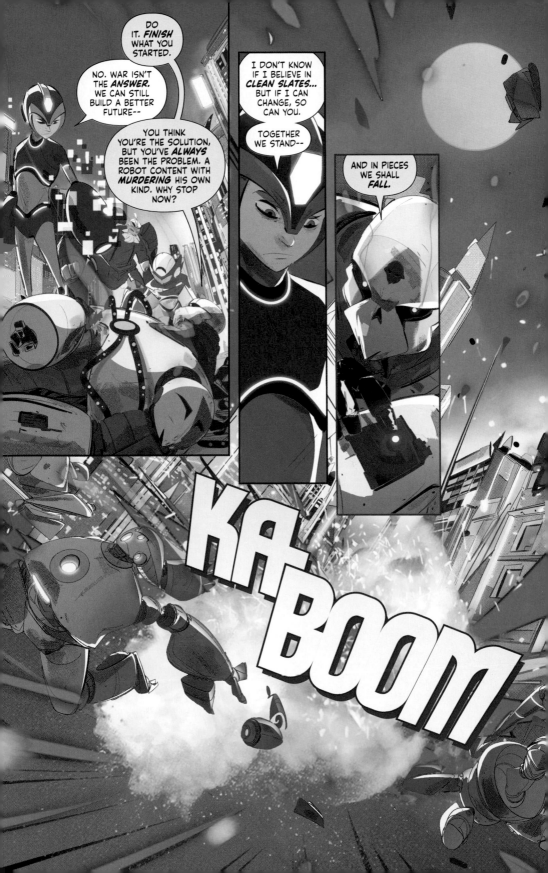

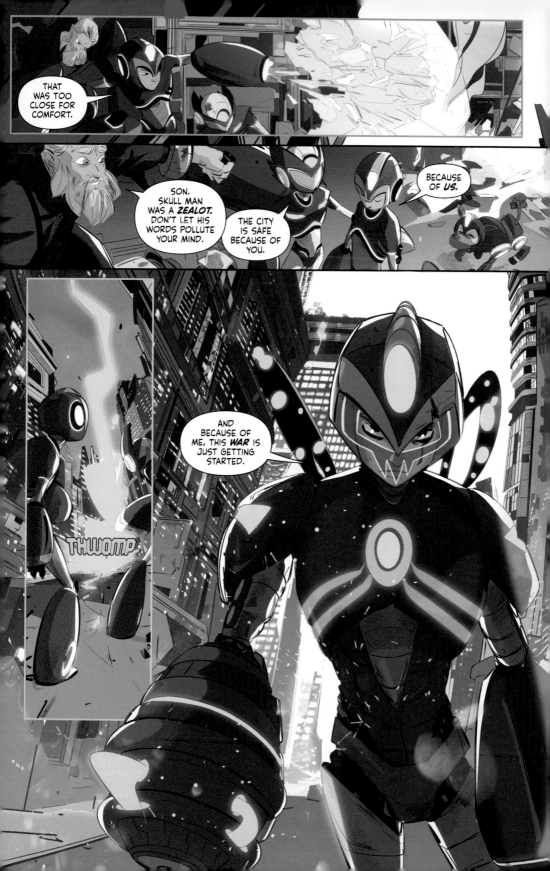

SO YOU CHOSE A SIDE AFTER ALL.
CHAPTER 5
I'M ON MY SIDE. AND MINE ALONE.
SON. PLEASE...

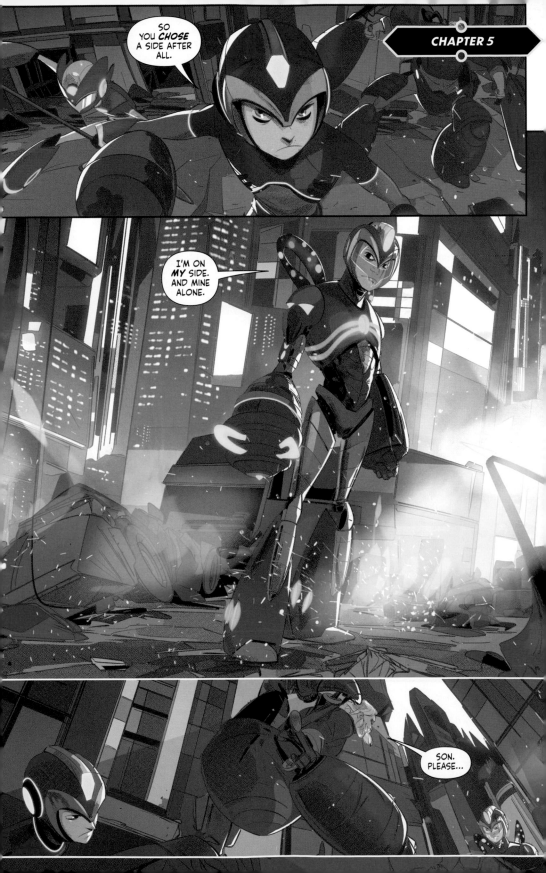

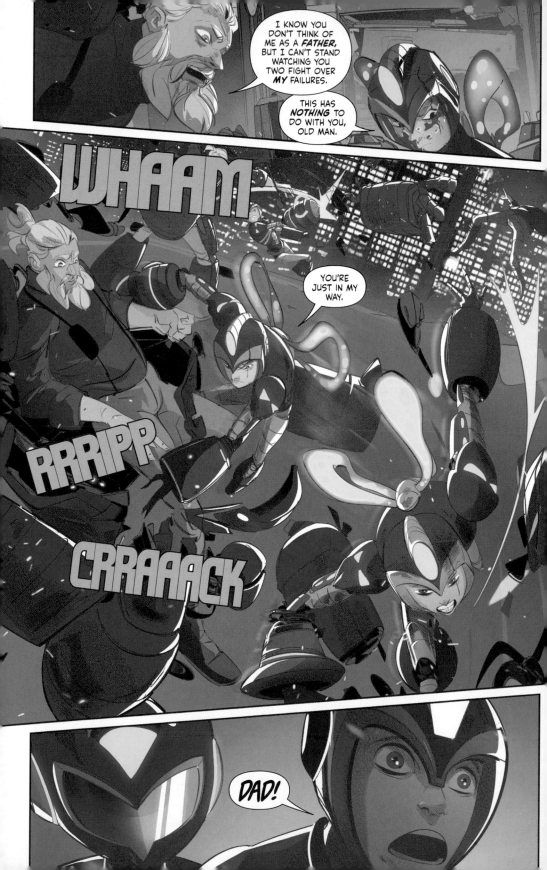

GET AWAY FROM HIM!
WITH PLEASURE.
SUNA, LOOK OUT!
GOOD TO KNOW THERE'S ONE SIBLING YOU WON'T SHOOT.
WHAP
POW
NOW!
KA-BLAM!

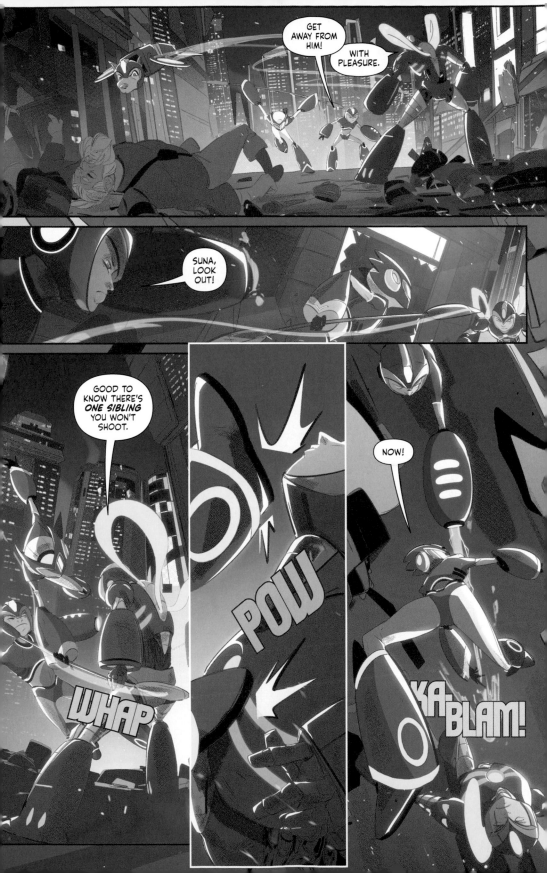

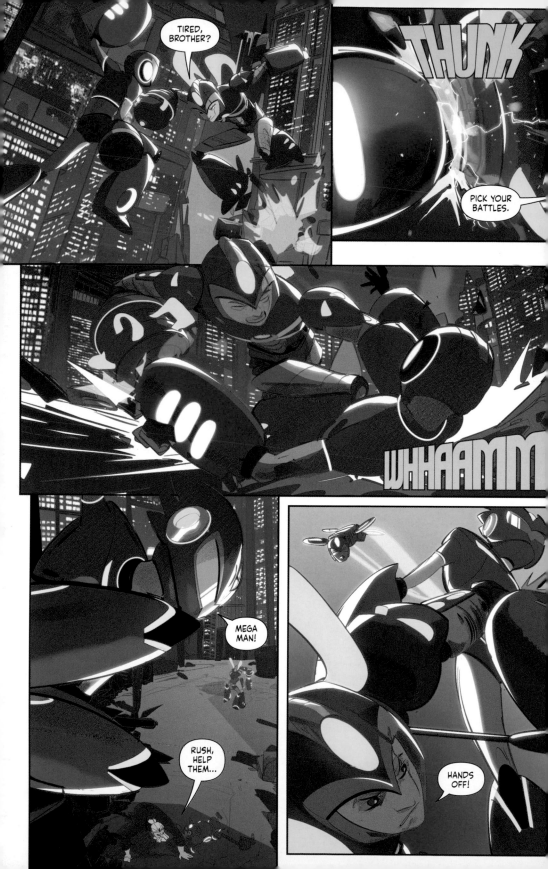

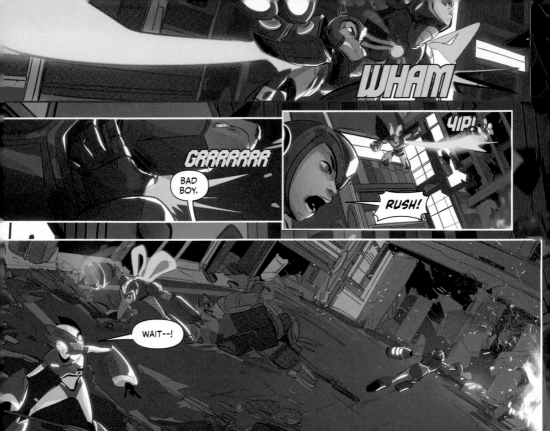

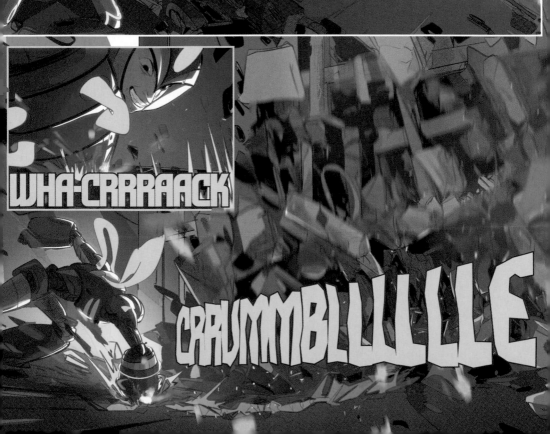

NOOOO!
CRRAAASH
I WON'T LET YOU **DESTROY** MY FAMILY.
I **NEVER** GOT ONE. WHY SHOULD YOU?
MEGA MAN ISN'T EVEN YOUR BLOOD.
SNAP
WHY FIGHT FOR HIM?

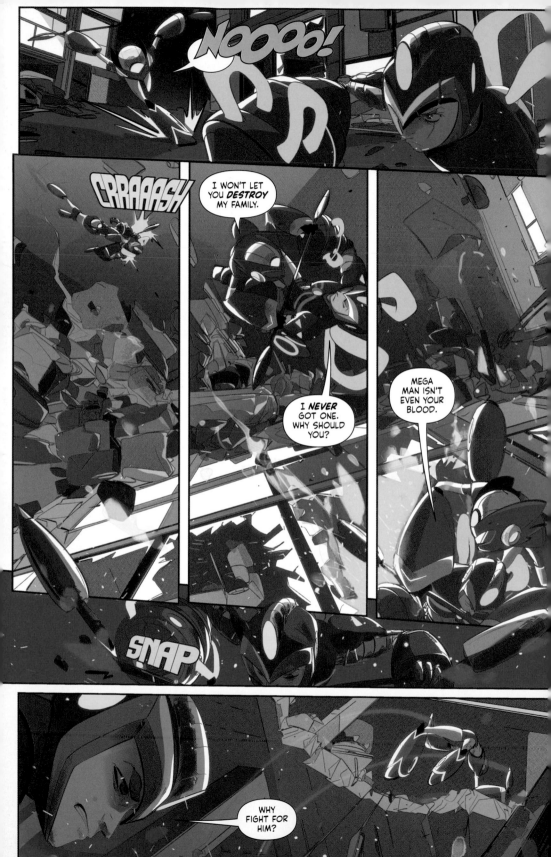

IT'S NOT ABOUT BLOOD.
YOU DON'T LOVE **YOUR FAMILY** BECAUSE YOU HAVE TO.
YOU LOVE THEM BECAUSE YOU ***CHOOSE TO.***

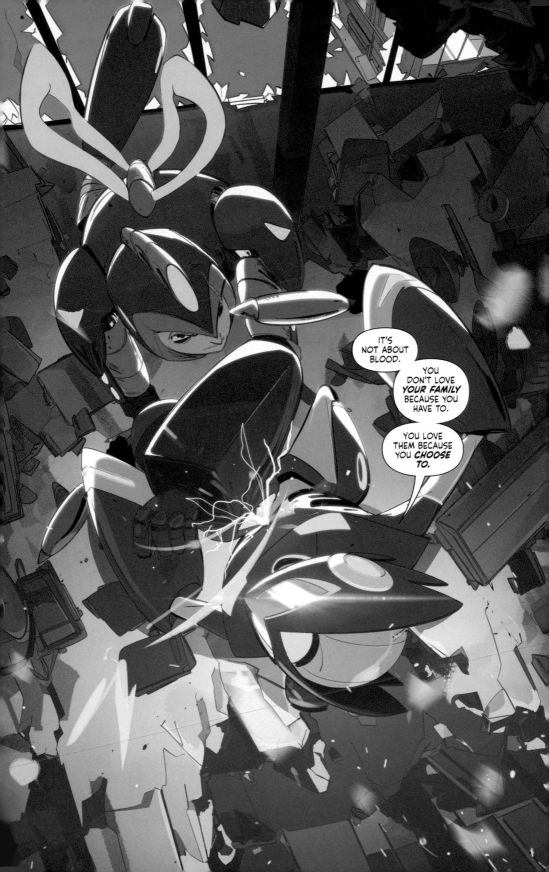

AND IF YOU CHOOSE TO *HATE* THEM?
IT'S BECAUSE HATING SOMEONE IS *EASIER* THAN BEING ALONE.
PAIN IS NEVER EASY.
LET ME GO!
KA-POW

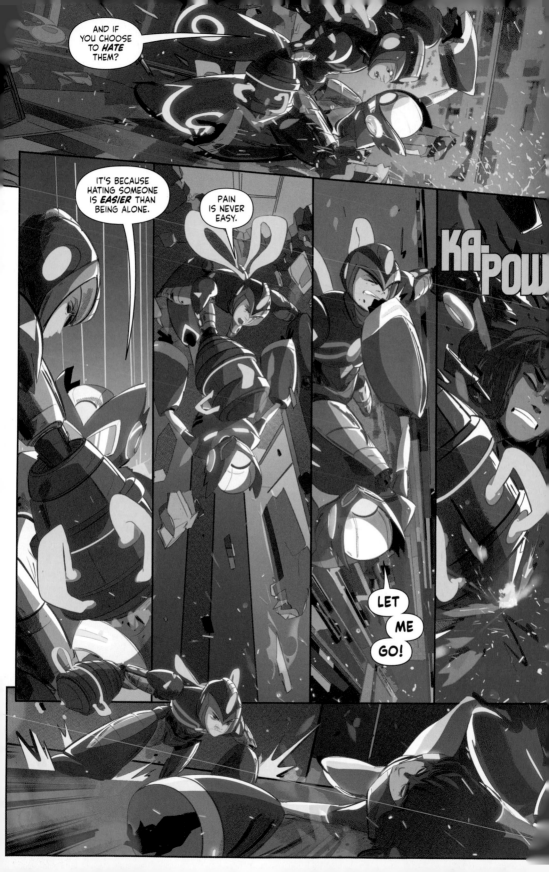

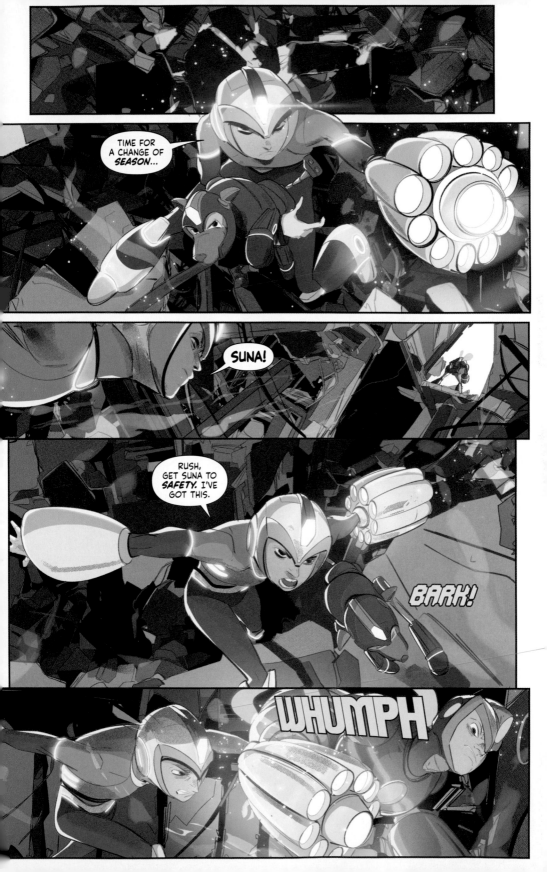

FEELING RESTED?
WHAM
NICE MAKEOVER, BY THE WAY. SKULL MAN LET YOU HAVE HIS SCHEMATICS? OR DID YOU GET 'EM SECONDHAND?
I MADE THE SAME DEAL YOU DID. AND UNLIKE YOU, I KNOW WHAT TO DO WITH IT.
OOOF!
CRAAAAAASH

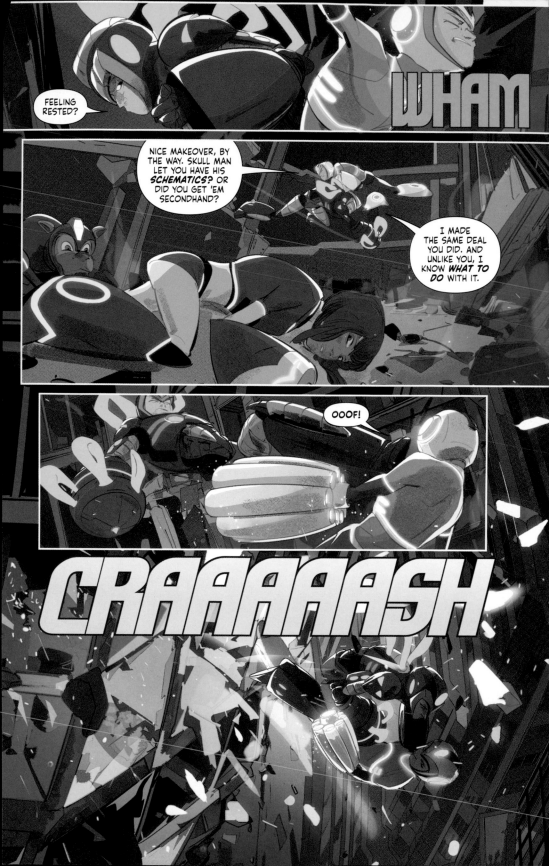

I WARNED YOU NOT TO PLAY HERO. YOU'RE TOO SOFT. ***TOO HUMAN.***
ROBOTS DESERVE A LEADER WHO SHOWS THEM THEIR ***POTENTIAL,*** NOT THEIR WEAKNESSES.
MINI, ACTIVATE ***AIR MAN SCHEMATICS!***
Comin' right up, chief! Emphasis on ***up!***

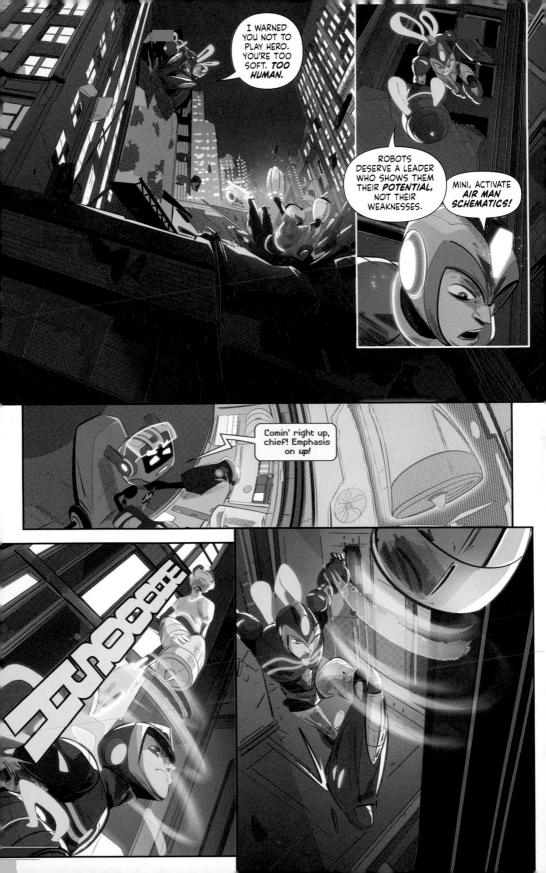

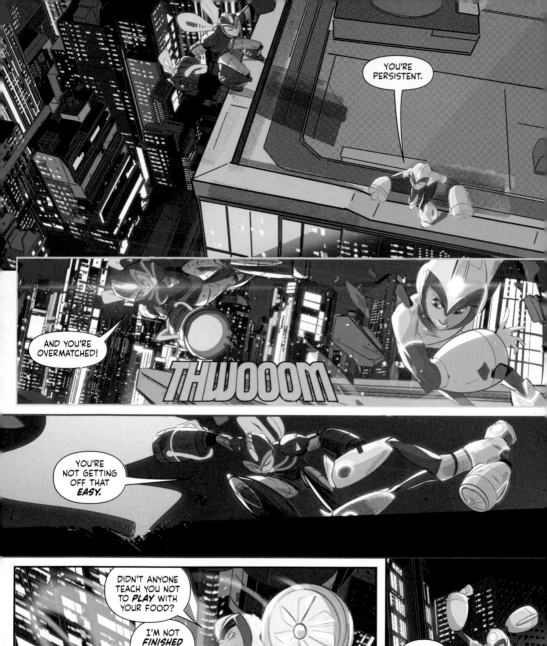

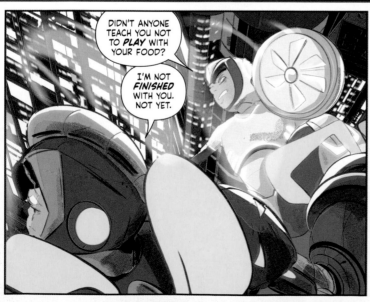

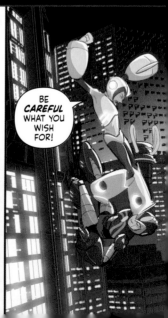

YOU DESERVE TO SUFFER.
WHAT DID I EVER DO TO YOU?
YOU STOLE MY LIFE.
I'VE ONLY EVER WANTED TO HELP YOU!
CRAAASH
OOOF!
EVERY NIGHT I DREAM OF A WORLD WHERE NIGHT HAD TAKEN YOU INSTEAD.
I WISH HE HAD NEVER TAKEN YOU.
DON'T LIE TO ME!
MINI, ACTIVATE FIRE MAN SCHEMATICS!

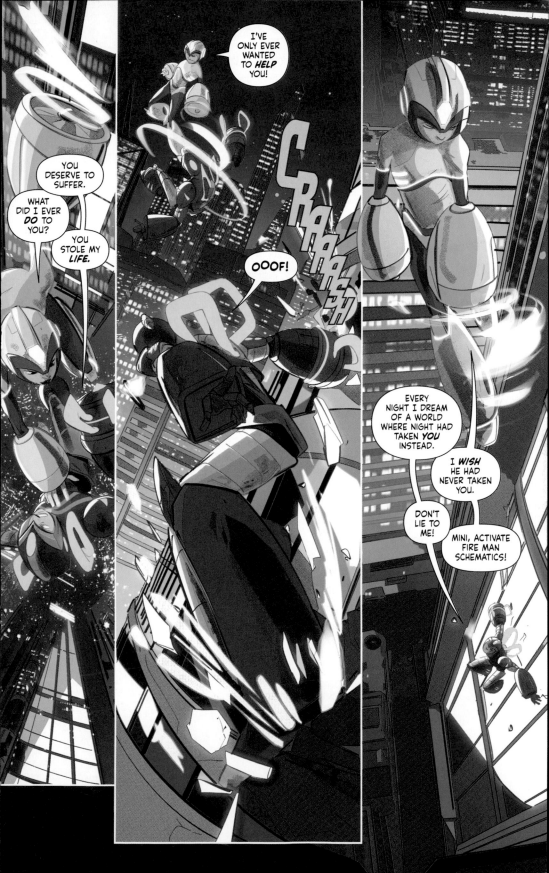

I DON'T WANT TO HURT YOU BUT YOU'RE GIVING ME NO CHOICE!
IS THAT ALL YOU GOT? YOU COULD NEVER HURT ME, BROTHER.
JUST.
GETTING.
STARTED!
MY TURN...
WHUMP
PATHETIC...
SON!
WE GOTTA DO SOMETHING.

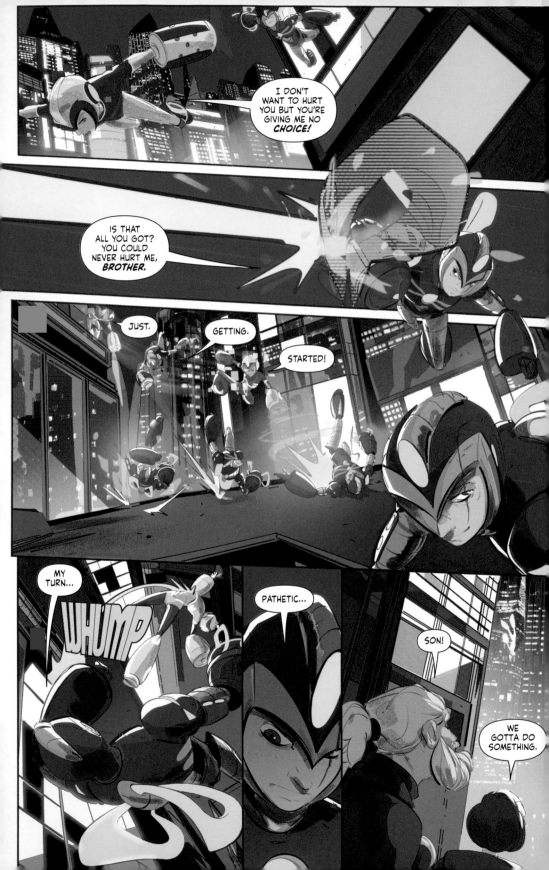

KRAAAAK
I'VE BEEN LOOKING FORWARD TO THIS MOMENT FOR A LONG TIME.
REVENGE WON'T TAKE THE PAIN AWAY!
HE'S RIGHT...
WHAT DO YOU KNOW ABOUT PAIN?
ALL YOUR LIFE, YOU'VE BEEN NOTHING BUT LOVED. YOUR FAMILY. YOUR FANS. AND LOOK WHERE IT GOT YOU.
WE LOVED YOU TOO, DAINI.
DON'T. DON'T SAY THAT.
WE DID. AND STILL DO. AFTER YOU DISAPPEARED, I LOOKED EVERYWHERE--
OBVIOUSLY NOT OR YOU WOULD HAVE DONE SOMETHING!
DON'T WORRY. THIS ISN'T REVENGE...
THIS IS A REBOOT!
NOT AGAIN!
WHAT IS THIS?
WHAT'S HAPPENING TO THEM?
THEY HAVE THE SAME PROGRAMMING...DAINI MUST HAVE TRIGGERED SOME KIND OF MEMORY FEEDBACK. AN ECHO...

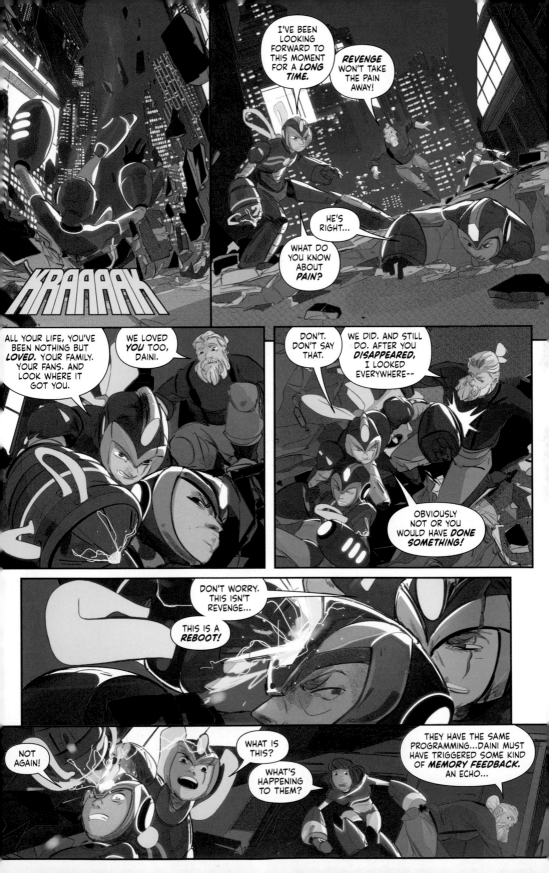

MEET YOUR TWIN BROTHER.
NEVER FORGET. TWO ARE BETTER THAN ONE. **TOGETHER** YOU CAN DO ANYTHING.
WELCOME HOME... SON.
IF YOU CAN'T HANDLE A TINY SCRATCH, YOU DON'T STAND A CHANCE AGAINST **MEGA MAN.**

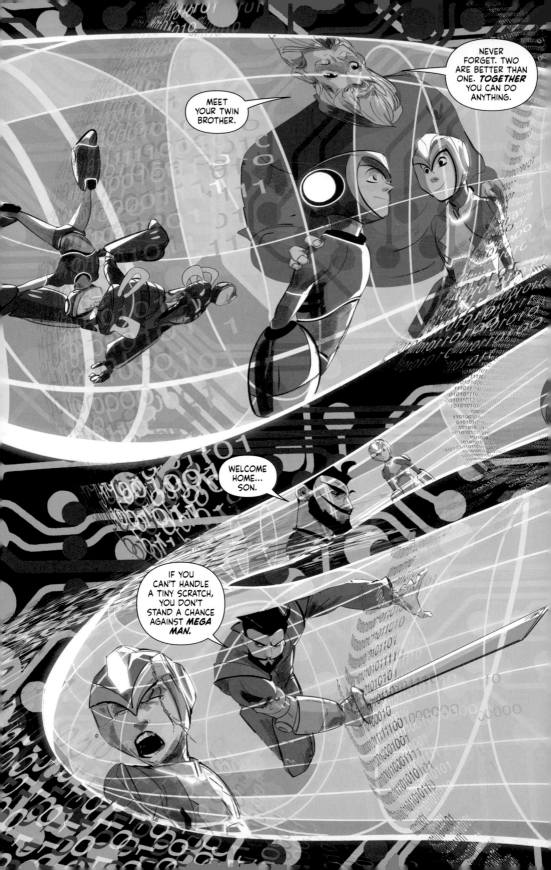

WHAT DO YOU WANT TO DO NEXT?
YOU PICK!
WHERE'S MY BROTHER?
I'M SORRY, AKI. HE'S *GONE.*
MAKE IT STOP!
I CAN'T!
EVERYONE FALLS, AKI, BUT *HEROES* ARE THE ONES THAT REFUSE TO STAY DOWN.
I HOPE HE'S OKAY.
HE WILL BE. IN *TIME.*
MEGA MAN *STOLE* MY LIFE. HE DESERVES EVERYTHING THAT'S COMING TO HIM...

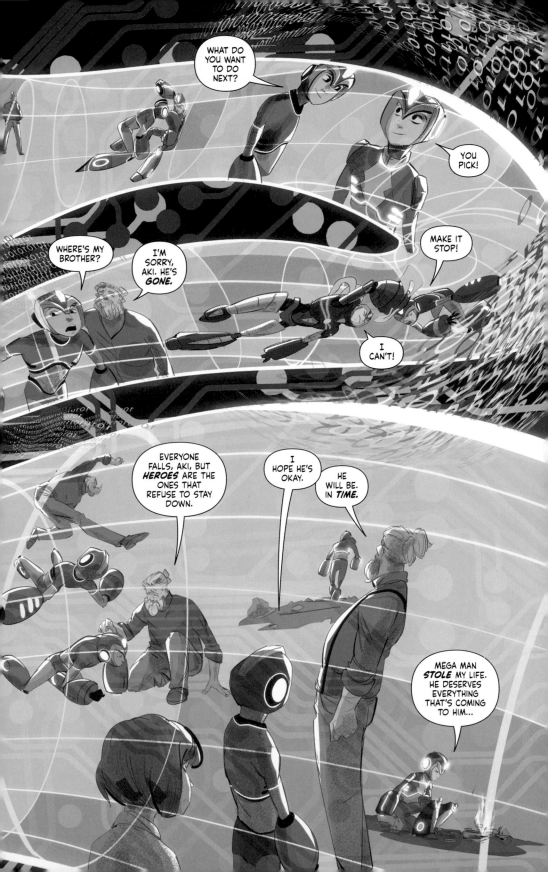

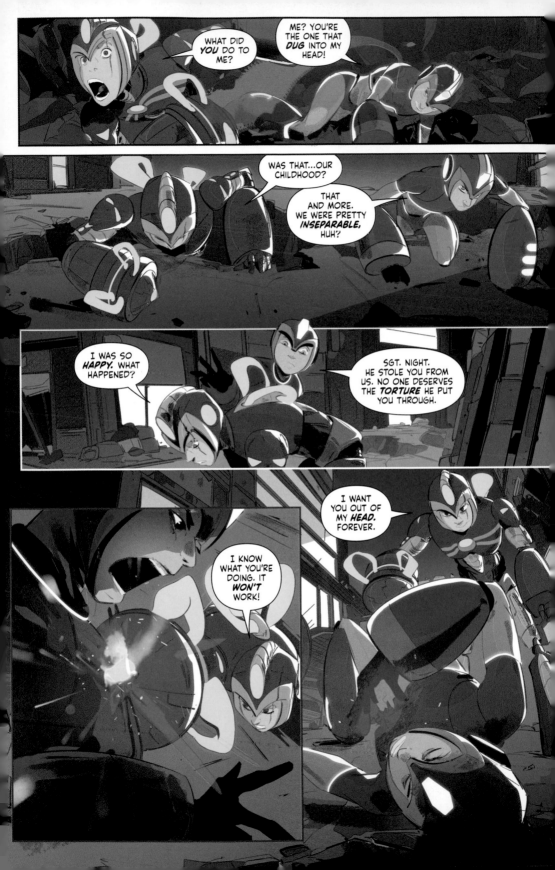

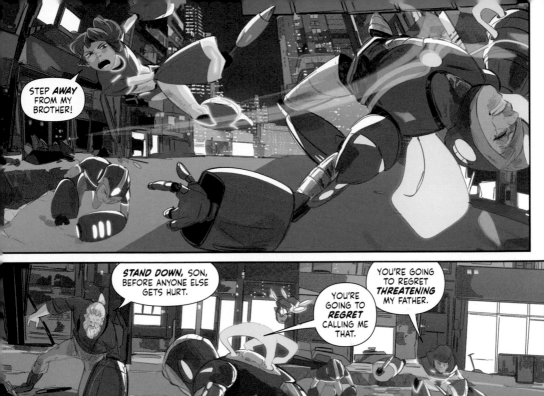

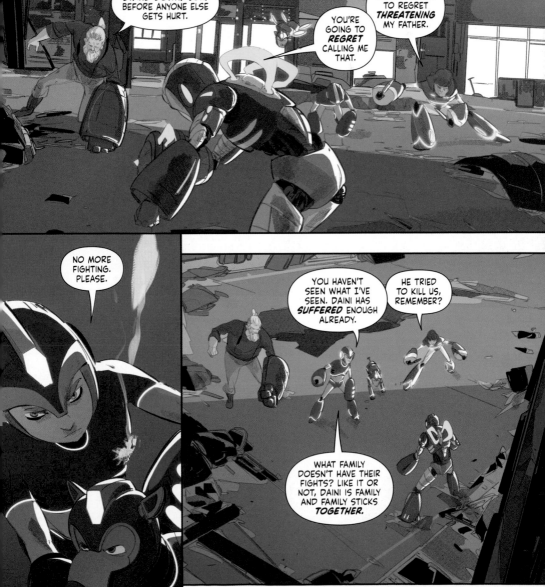

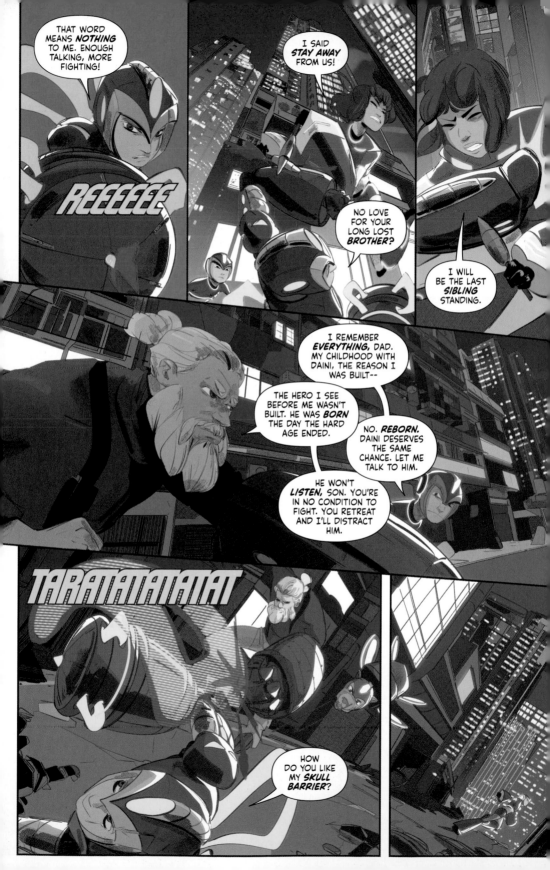

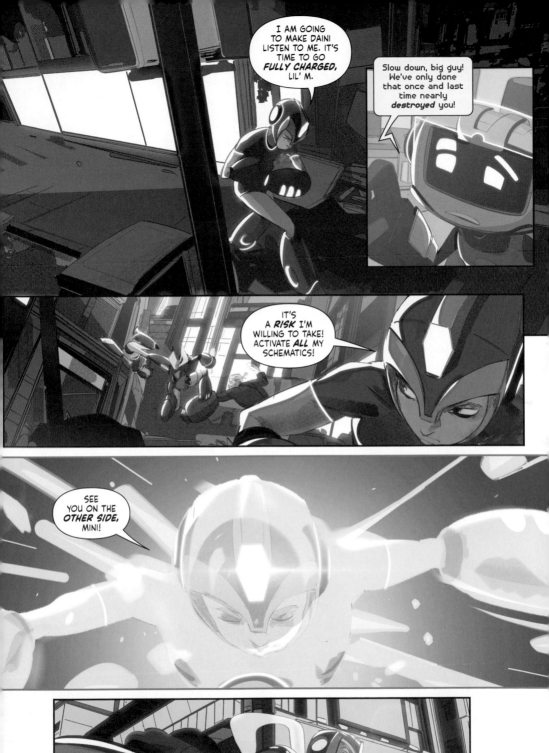
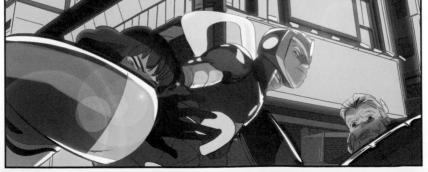

LET'S SETTLE THIS *FAMILY FEUD* ONCE AND FOR ALL.

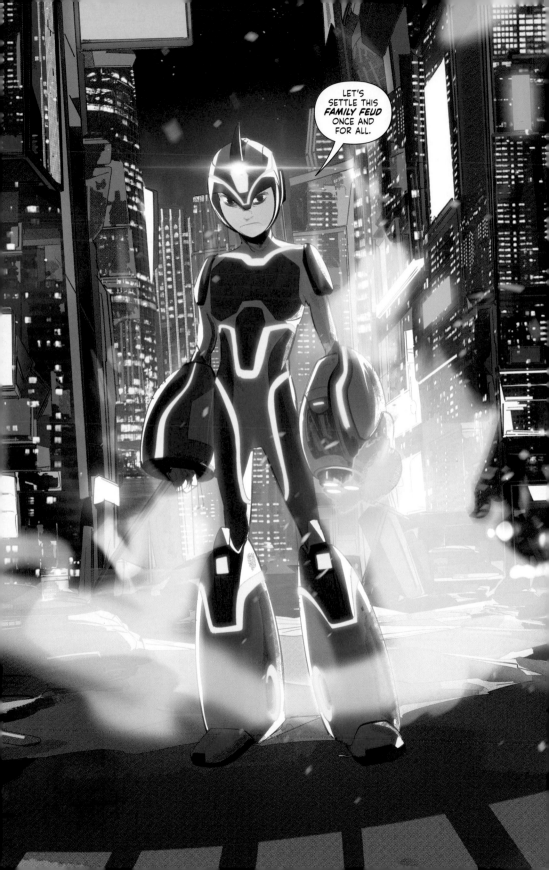

CHAPTER 6
HOW DID WE END UP *HERE?*
FOR THE SECOND TIME THIS YEAR, SILICON CITY ALMOST FELL. SOME OF US TOOK *A STAND.* ON BOTH SIDES.
FIRST I WAS *A WEAPON.* THEN I GOT TO BE A KID...
NOW I'M READY TO BE *A HERO.*

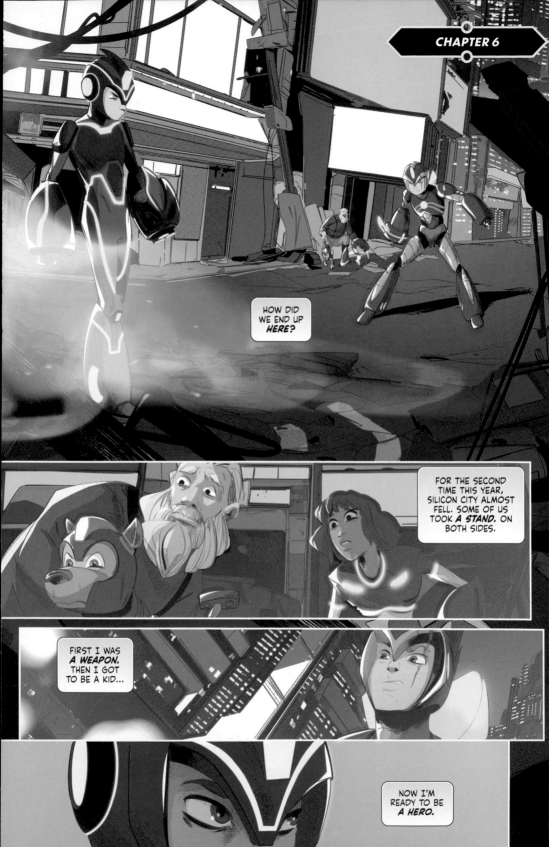

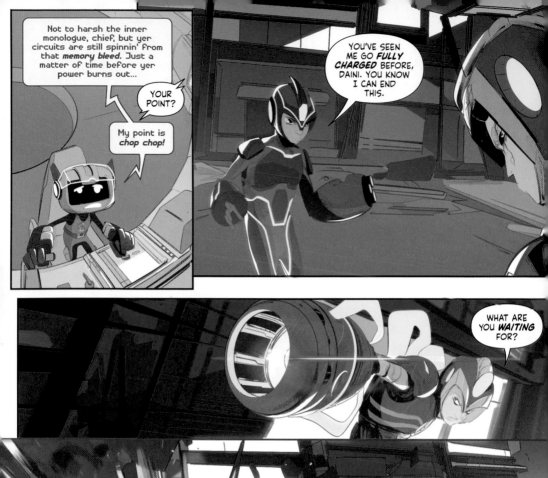

Not to harsh the inner monologue, chief, but yer circuits are still spinnin' from that *memory bleed*. Just a matter of time before yer power burns out...

YOUR POINT?

My point is *chop chop!*

YOU'VE SEEN ME GO *FULLY CHARGED* BEFORE, DAINI. YOU KNOW I CAN END THIS.

WHAT ARE YOU *WAITING* FOR?

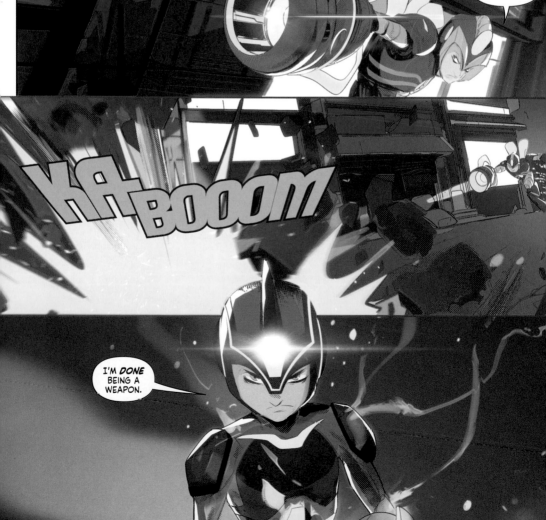

KA BOOOM

I'M *DONE* BEING A WEAPON.

I'M NOT!
SHKRRRRAK
WANNA TRY TALKING INSTEAD?
WHAAM
NO THANKS.

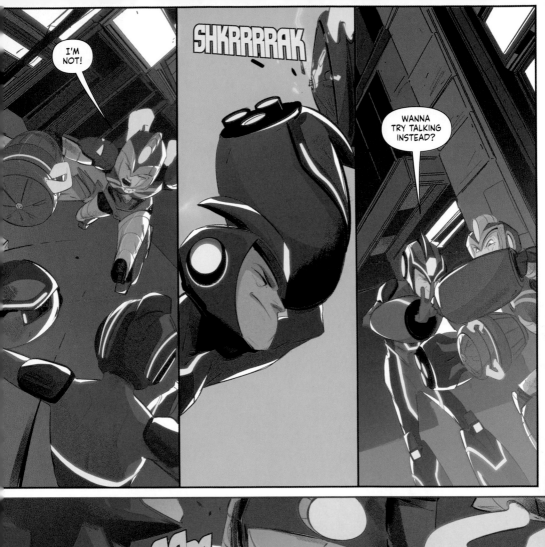

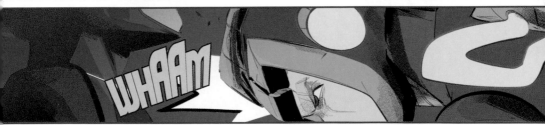

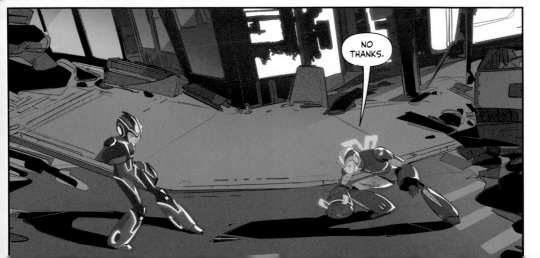

YOUR CHOICE.
FWWOOOOOM
IF THIS IS ALL THE FIGHT YOU HAVE LEFT--
--WHY KEEP FIGHTING?
WHOOOOOOOSH
THUD

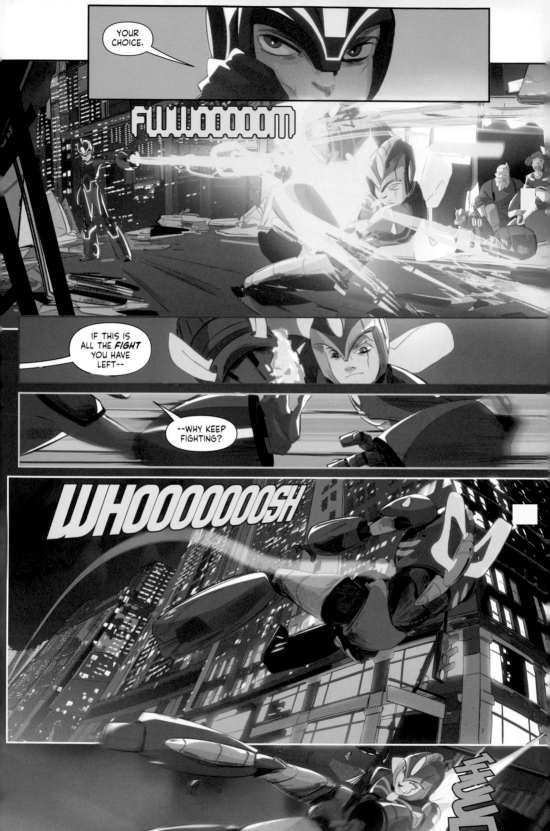

THERE IT IS AGAIN. THAT KILLER INSTINCT...
I TOLD YOU, I WON'T DESTROY MY OWN BROTHER.
BUT YOU COULD. AND YOU LOVE THAT.
DON'T--
I KNOW BECAUSE I'VE FELT IT TOO. KNOWING YOU HAVE THAT POWER, IT ALMOST MAKES YOU FEEL WHOLE.
ALL YOU HAVE TO DO NOW IS USE IT.
STAY DOWN, DAINI...
WHOMMMMP
I SAID STAY. DOWN.

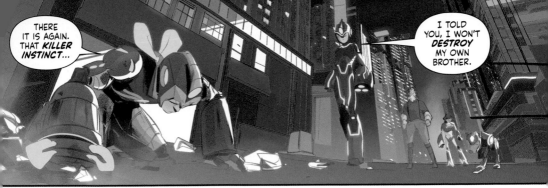

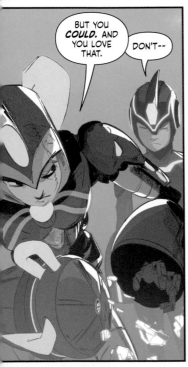

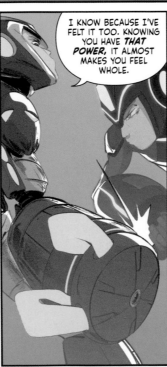

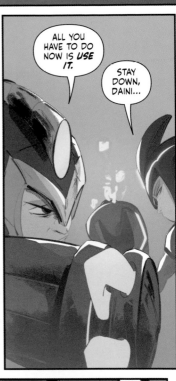

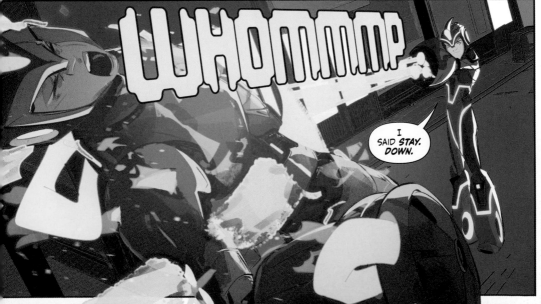

YOU WANT TO SAY WE'RE NOTHING ALIKE, BUT WE BOTH KNOW THAT'S NOT TRUE.
THEN THERE'S STILL HOPE FOR YOU. FOR US.
SAY IT ALL YOU WANT...
BUT AS LONG AS YOU LET ME LIVE, I'LL NEVER LET YOU BELIEVE IT.
Waitaminute, Big M--

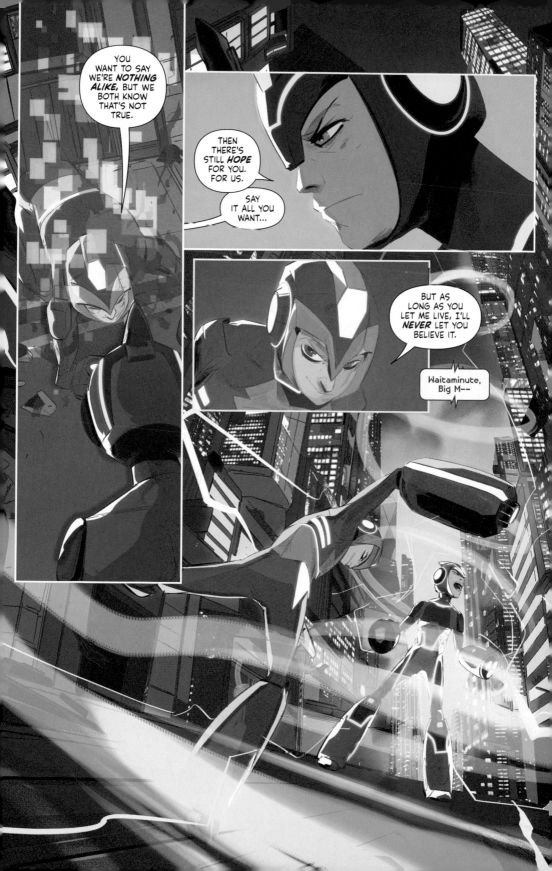

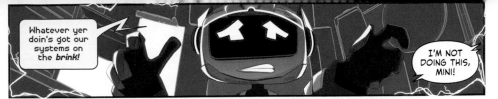

Whatever yer doin's got our systems on the *brink!*

I'M NOT DOING THIS, MINI!

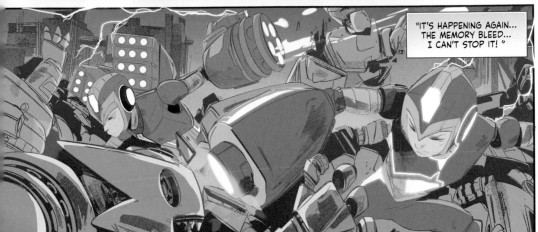

"IT'S HAPPENING AGAIN... THE MEMORY BLEED... I CAN'T STOP IT! "

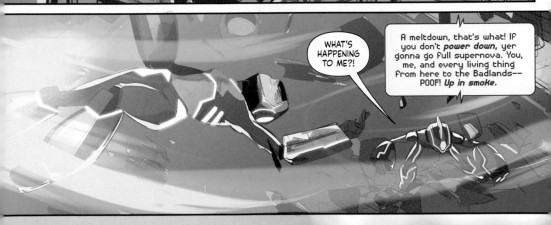

WHAT'S HAPPENING TO ME?!

A meltdown, that's what! If you don't *power down,* yer gonna go full supernova. You, me, and every living thing from here to the Badlands-- POOF! *Up in smoke.*

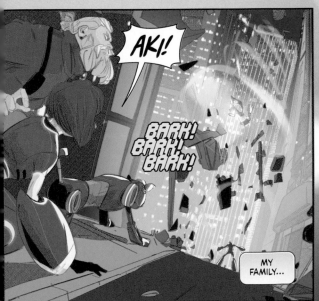

AKI!

BARK! BARK! BARK!

MY FAMILY...

Listen to me, Big M. I can't disengage schematics until you *ease off* the throttle.

Yer feelin' a lot of *feelings* right now. And that's okay.

I know what you've been through. I'm sorry I couldn't be there every step of the way. But I'm *here* now.

You risked yer neck to bring me back. Now lemme return *the favor.*

Take a deep breath.
For every bad memory...
There's a happy one, too.
Gotcha!

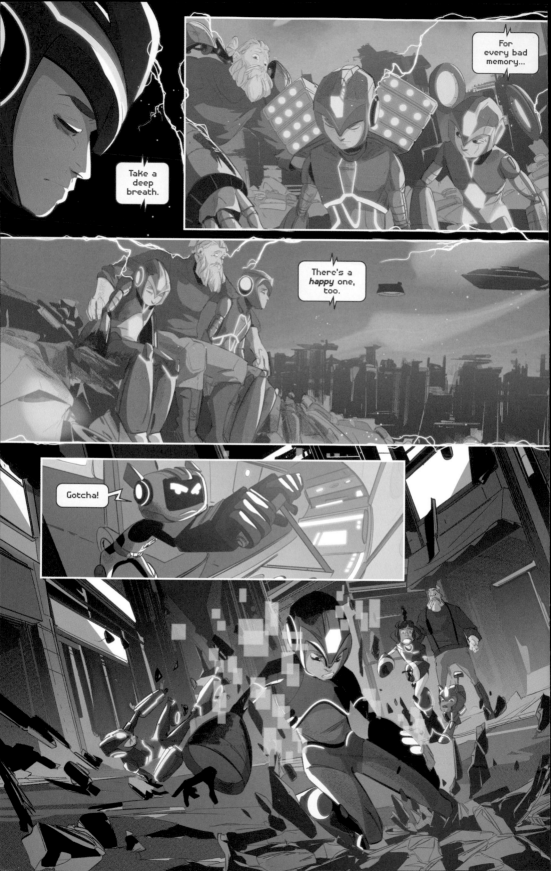

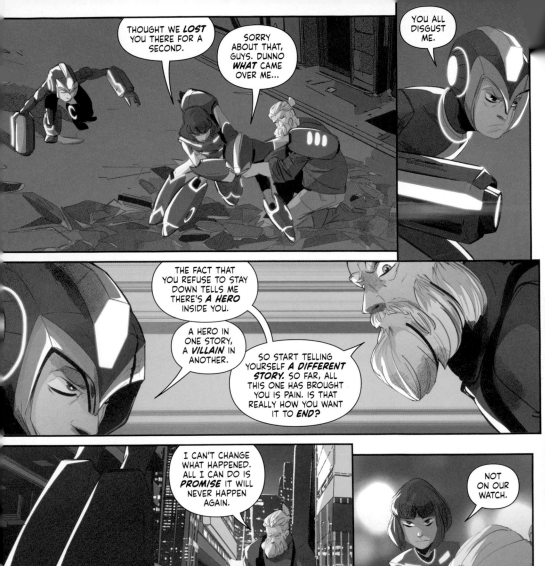

THOUGHT WE *LOST* YOU THERE FOR A SECOND.

SORRY ABOUT THAT, GUYS. DUNNO *WHAT* CAME OVER ME...

YOU ALL DISGUST ME.

THE FACT THAT YOU REFUSE TO STAY DOWN TELLS ME THERE'S *A HERO* INSIDE YOU.

A HERO IN ONE STORY, A *VILLAIN* IN ANOTHER.

SO START TELLING YOURSELF *A DIFFERENT STORY.* SO FAR, ALL THIS ONE HAS BROUGHT YOU IS PAIN. IS THAT REALLY HOW YOU WANT IT TO *END?*

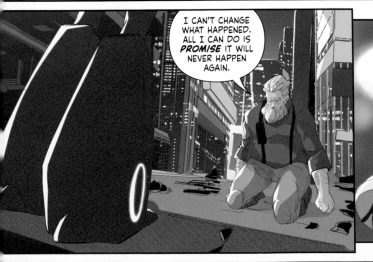

I CAN'T CHANGE WHAT HAPPENED. ALL I CAN DO IS *PROMISE* IT WILL NEVER HAPPEN AGAIN.

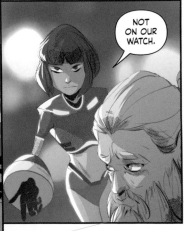

NOT ON OUR WATCH.

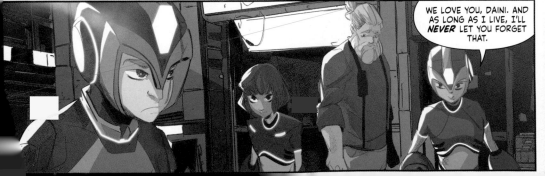

WE LOVE YOU, DAINI. AND AS LONG AS I LIVE, I'LL *NEVER* LET YOU FORGET THAT.

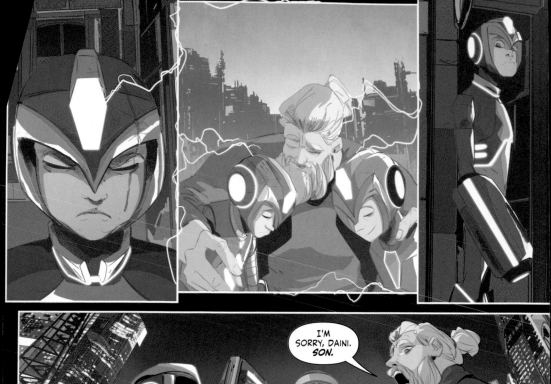

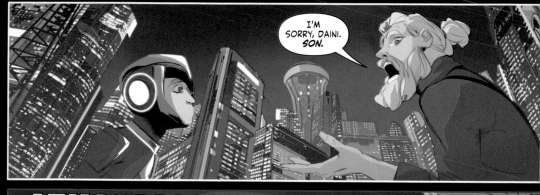

I'M SORRY, DAINI. *SON.*

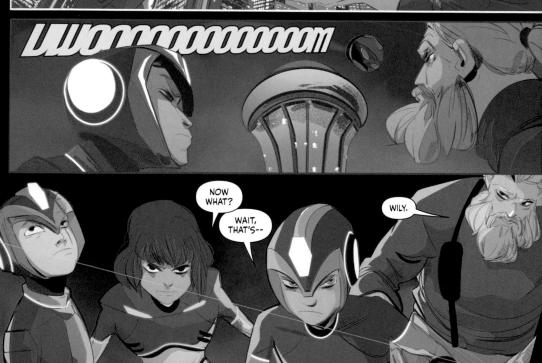

UWOmmmmooooooom

NOW WHAT?

WAIT, THAT'S--

WILY.

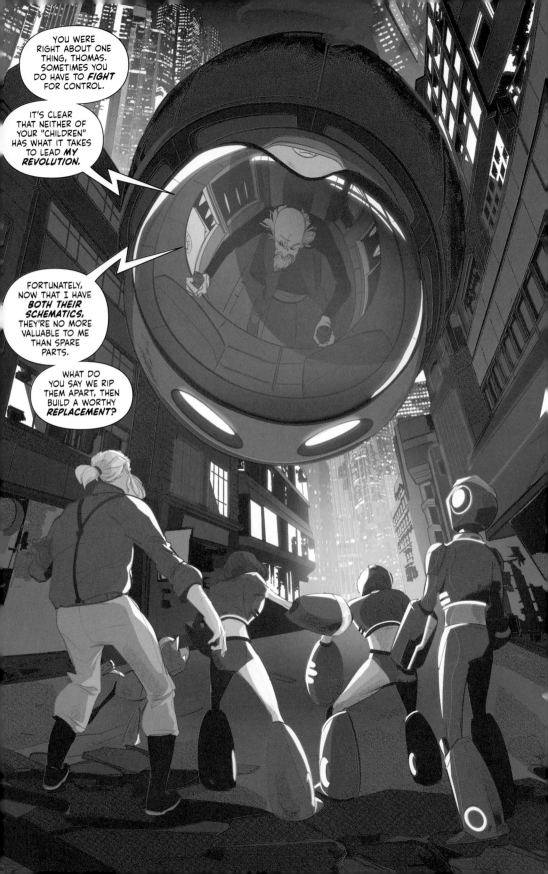

I'M AFRAID I DISAGREE, ALBERT. YOU WERE ALWAYS A LITTLE MACABRE FOR MY TASTE.
IT WAS A RHETORICAL QUESTION. YOU DON'T HAVE A SAY IN THE MATTER.
BIG TALK FOR A SMALL MAN HIDING BEHIND MACHINES AND ROBOTS.
YOU DON'T STAND A CHANCE, WILY.
THWOOOOM
THWOOOOOM
STAND A CHANCE? HA! WHEN I'M THROUGH WITH YOU, YOU WON'T BE STANDING AT ALL!

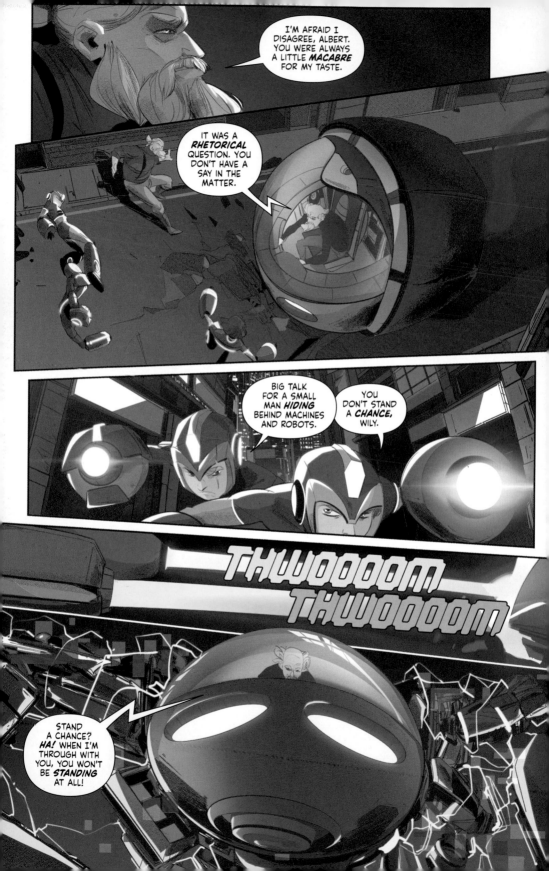

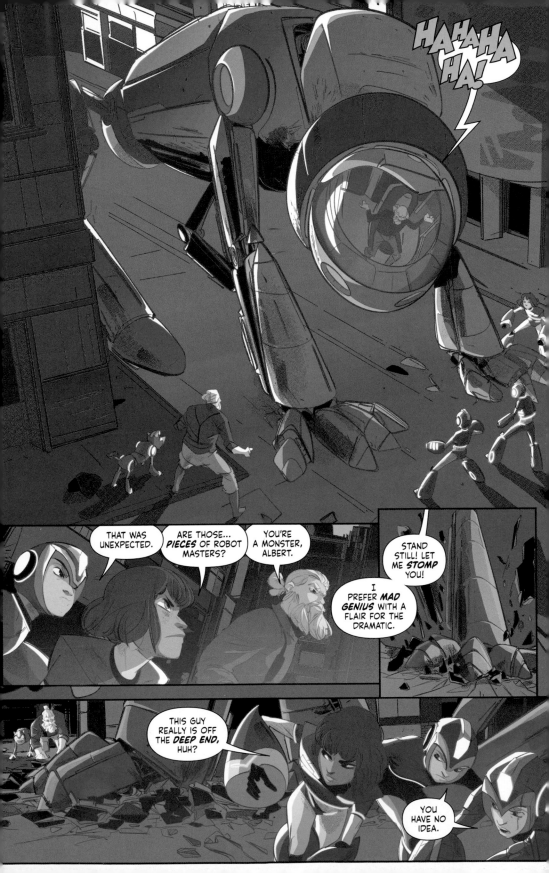

RUN, HIDE... MUST WE GO THROUGH THE RIGMAROLE?
I'VE WAITED FOR THIS MOMENT SINCE THE HARD AGE. PEACE HAS TURNED YOU INTO A HYPOCRITE, BOT'S BANE. YOU FORGOT OUR OBJECTIVE.
PUPPETING FROM THE SHADOWS? THAT WAS YOUR OBJECTIVE, NOT MINE.
HUSH NOW. I'M HERE TO SPARE YOU THE TRAUMA OF WATCHING ME DISMANTLE YOUR OWN BROOD. TRULY THE LEAST I CAN DO.
AHHHHHHH!
DAD! NO!
LET HIM GO! NOW!
SO HE DOES CARE...

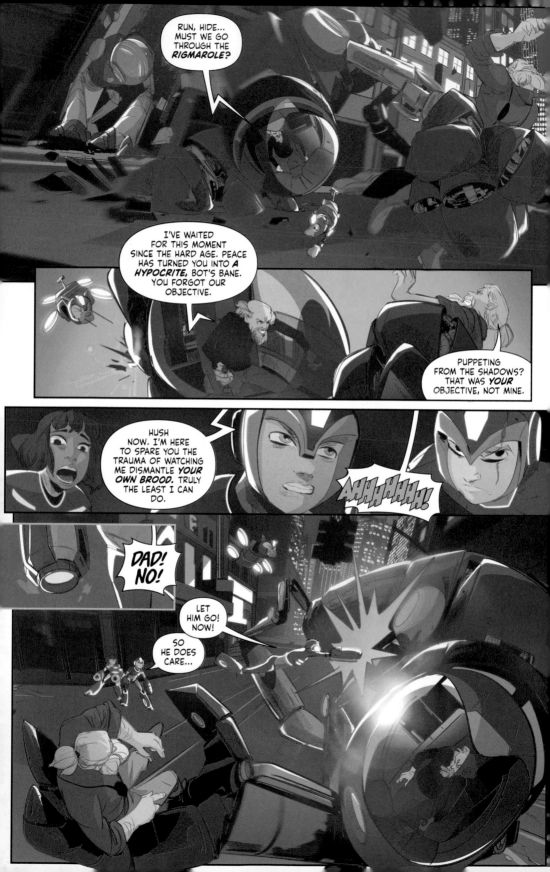

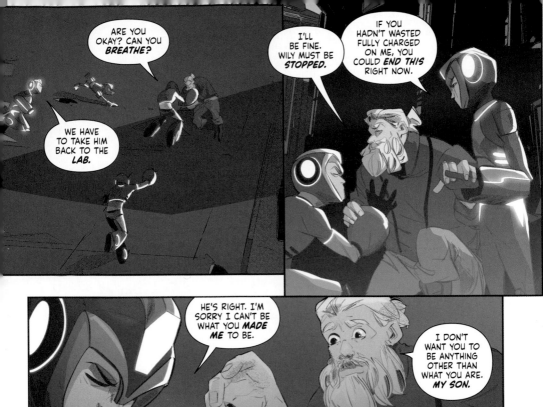

ARE YOU OKAY? CAN YOU *BREATHE*?

WE HAVE TO TAKE HIM BACK TO THE *LAB.*

I'LL BE FINE. WILY MUST BE *STOPPED.*

IF YOU HADN'T WASTED FULLY CHARGED ON ME, YOU COULD *END THIS* RIGHT NOW.

HE'S RIGHT. I'M SORRY I CAN'T BE WHAT YOU *MADE ME* TO BE.

I DON'T WANT YOU TO BE ANYTHING OTHER THAN WHAT YOU ARE. *MY SON.*

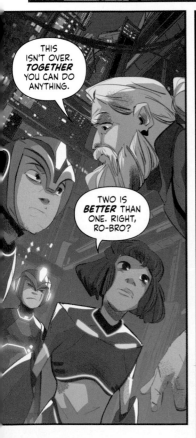

THIS ISN'T OVER. *TOGETHER* YOU CAN DO ANYTHING.

TWO IS *BETTER* THAN ONE. RIGHT, RO-BRO?

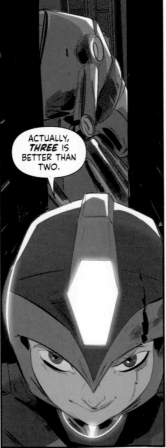

ACTUALLY, *THREE* IS BETTER THAN TWO.

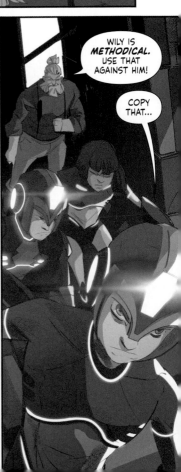

WILY IS *METHODICAL.* USE THAT AGAINST HIM!

COPY THAT...

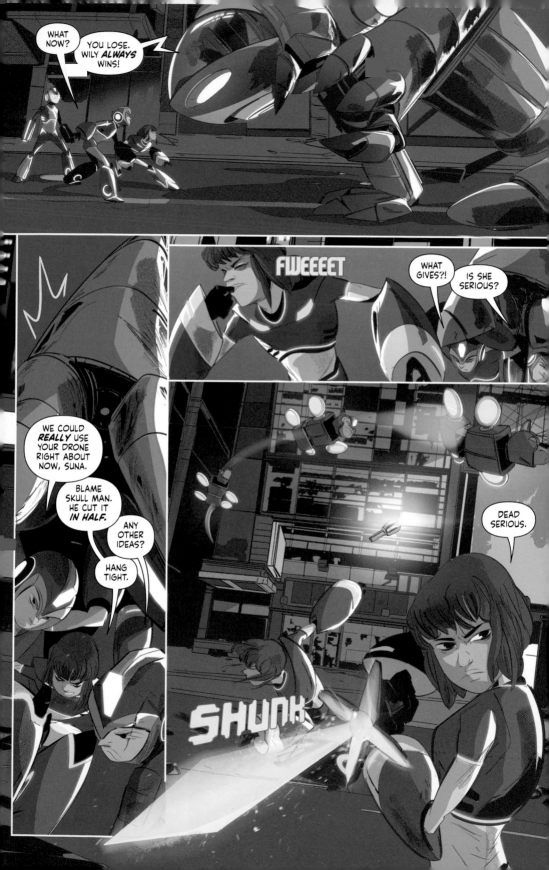

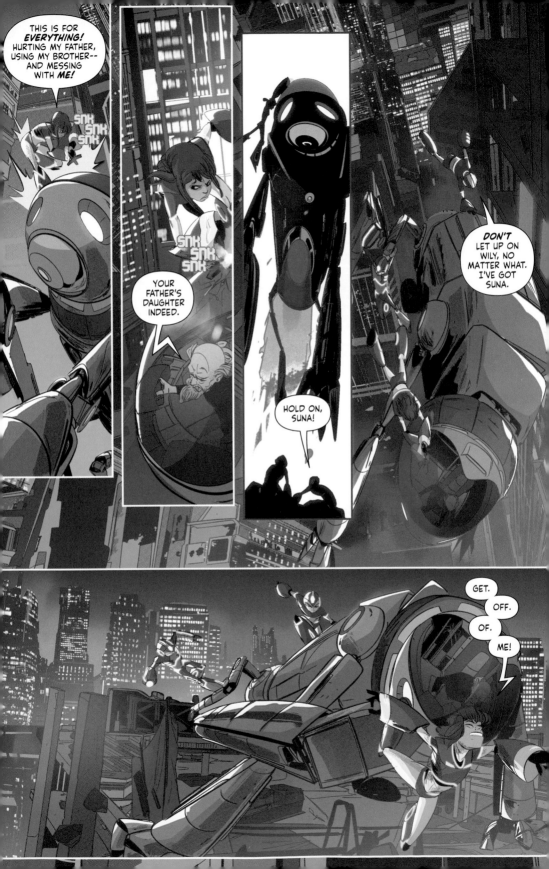

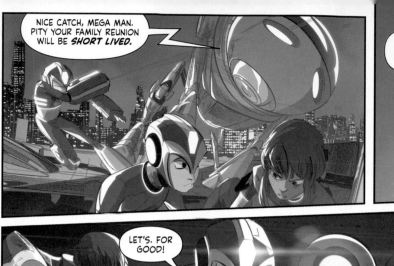

NICE CATCH, MEGA MAN. PITY YOUR FAMILY REUNION WILL BE *SHORT LIVED.*

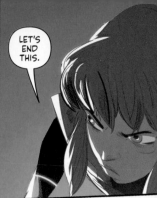

LET'S END THIS.

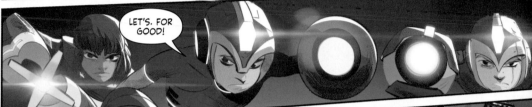

LET'S. FOR GOOD!

THWOM WOM WOM WOM

IM-IM-IMPOSSIBLE!!

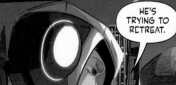

HE'S TRYING TO RETREAT.

WE *CAN'T* LET HIM GET AWAY!

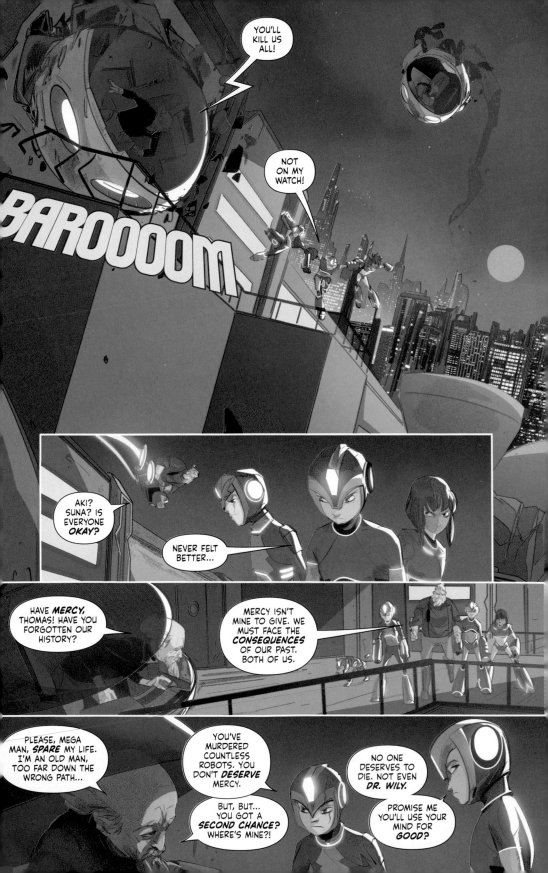

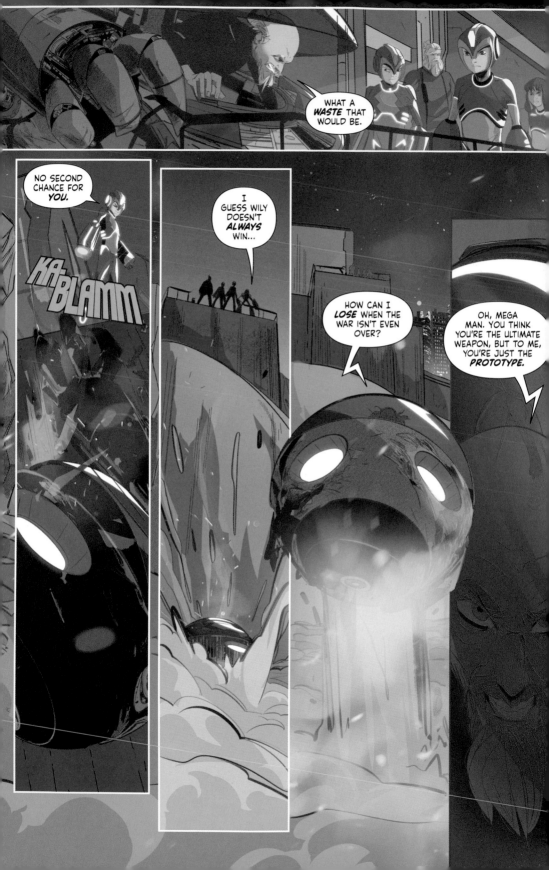

I GUESS THANKS ARE IN ORDER. YOU REALLY SAVED US BACK THERE.
YOU LET WILY GET AWAY.
NO MATTER HOW HARD YOU TRY... WE'LL NEVER BE BROTHERS.
YOUR ACTIONS SAY OTHERWISE.
UNTIL WE MEET AGAIN. BROTHER.

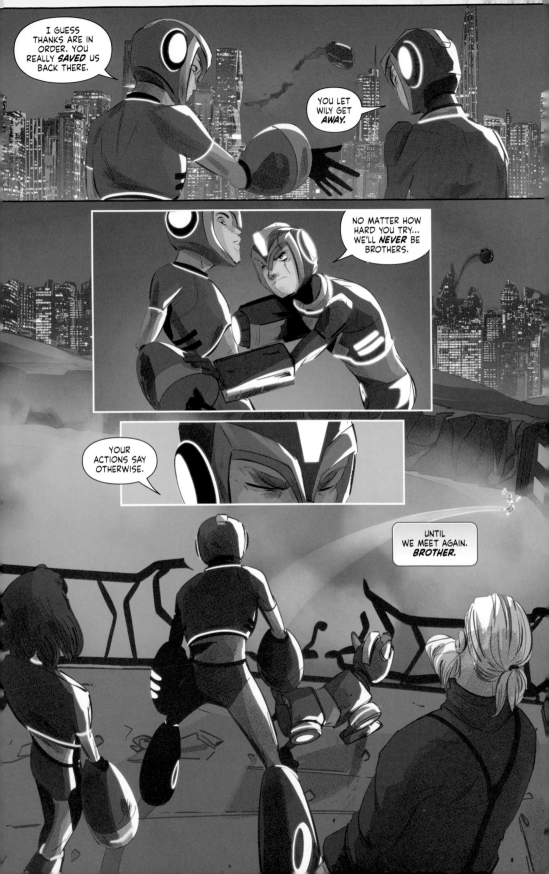

THANKS FOR STAYING IN MY WAY, SIS.
ALWAYS.
I COULDN'T BE MORE PROUD.
I'M SORRY, DAD...FOR EVERYTHING.
I'M THE ONE THAT SHOULD BE SORRY. M SECRETS DROVE YO TO THAT MADMAN.
AND I TURNED MY BACK ON MY OWN FAMILY. BUT NEVER AGAIN.
WHY THE LONG FACE, FAM? WE JUST WON!
FOR NOW. WITH THE DATA WILY HAS STOLEN, IT'S ONLY A MATTER OF TIME BEFORE HE STRIKES AGAIN.
AND WHEN HE DOES, WE'LL BE READY.
END

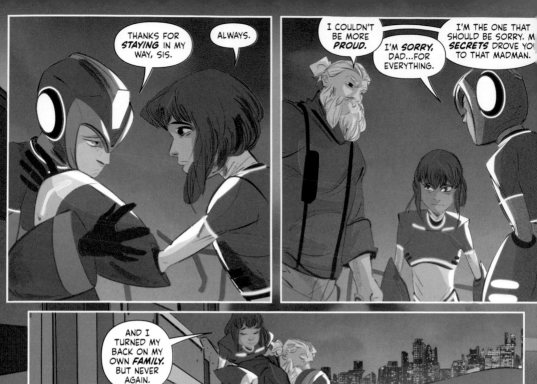

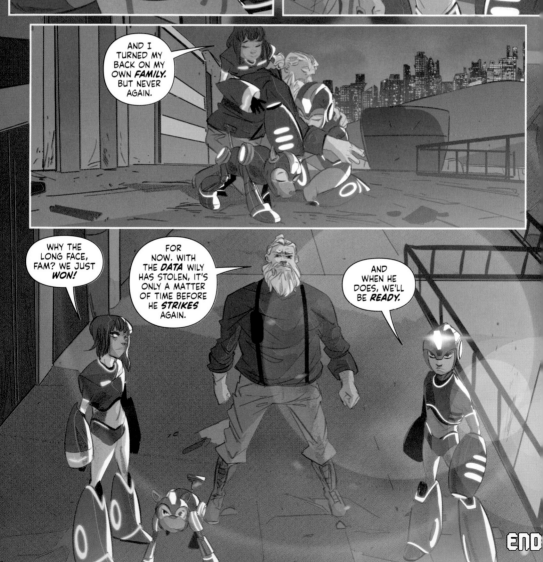

COVER GALLERY

ISSUE #1 COVER BY **TONI INFANTE**

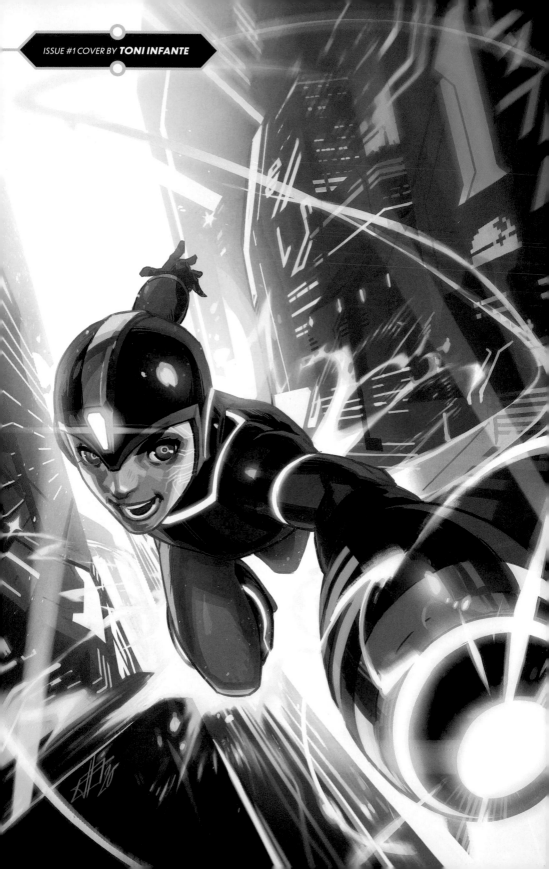

ISSUE #2 COVER BY **TONI INFANTE**

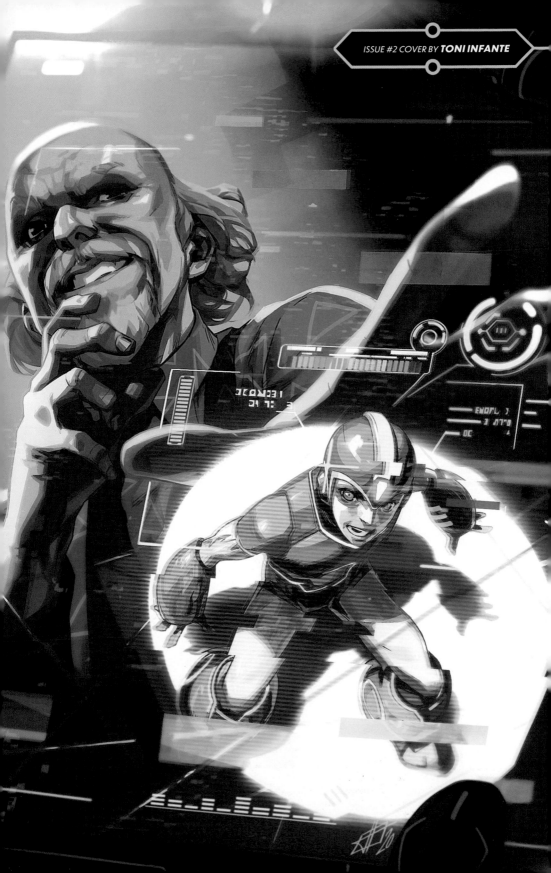

ISSUE #3 COVER BY **TONI INFANTE**

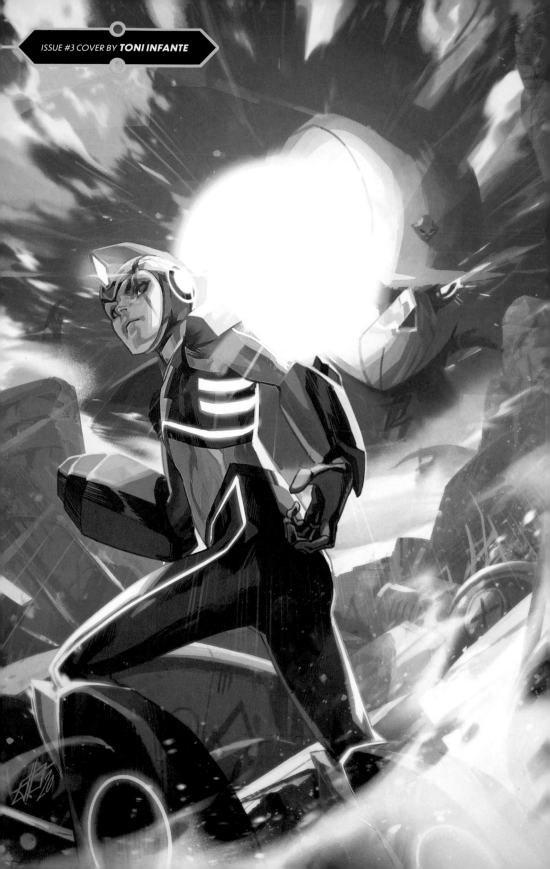

ISSUE #4 COVER BY **TONI INFANTE**

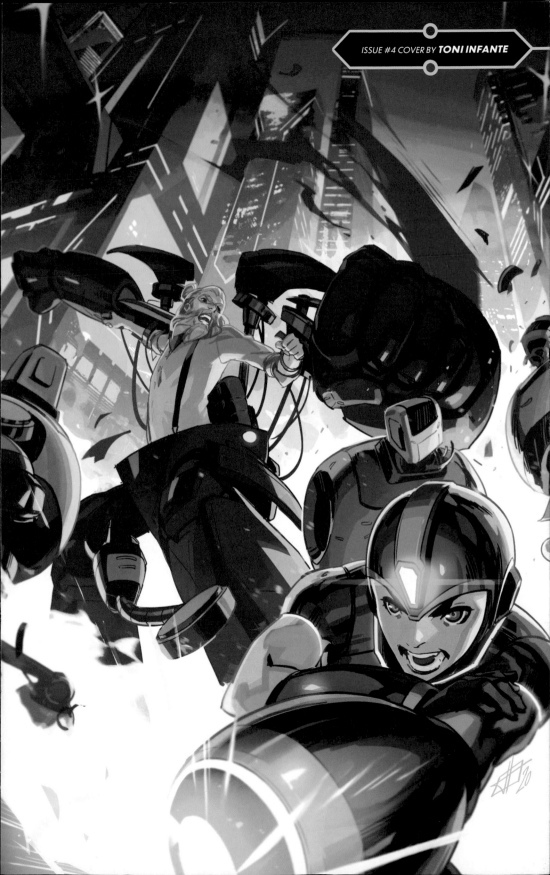

ISSUE #5 COVER BY **TONI INFANTE**

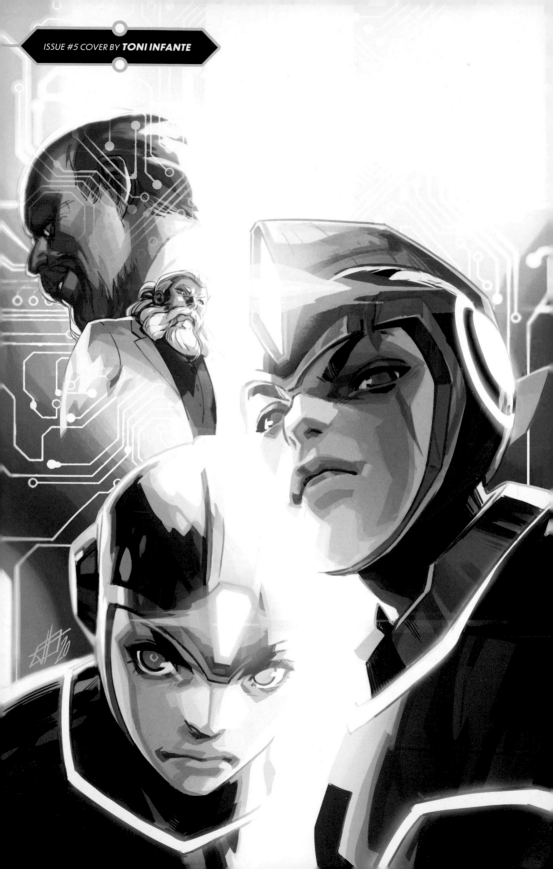

ISSUE #6 COVER BY **TONI INFANTE**

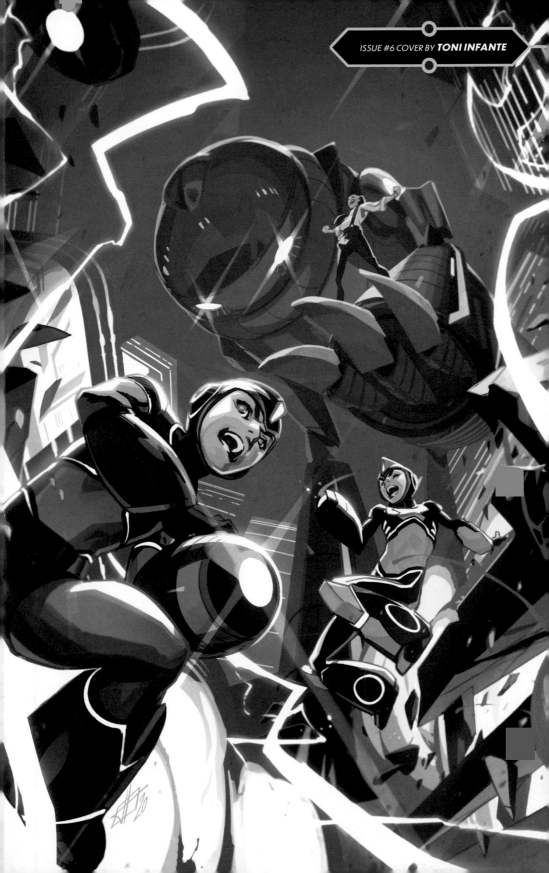

DISCOVER
EXCITING NEW WORLDS

New York Times Bestselling Author
JUST BEYOND
THE SCARE SCHOOL

Sam Davies
Hex Vet
Witches in Training

S.M. Vidaurri
All My Friends Are Ghosts
Hannah Krieger

NEW YORK TIMES BESTSELLER
ART BALTAZAR
DREW AND JOT
DUELING DOODLES

SPACE BEAR
ETHAN YOUNG

MARIE SPÉNALE
WONDER PONY

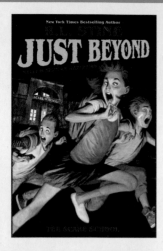

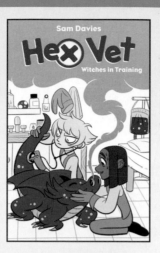

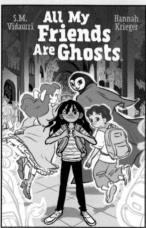

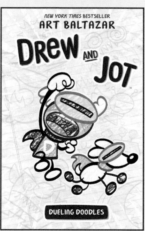

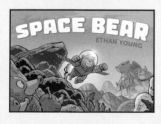

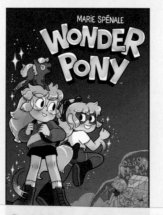

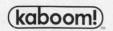

Just Beyond
R.L. Stine, Kelly & Nichole Matthews
Just Beyond: The Scare School
ISBN: 9781684154166 | $9.99 US
Just Beyond: The Horror at Happy Landings
ISBN: 9781684155477 | $9.99 US
Just Beyond: Welcome to Beast Island
ISBN: 978-1-68415-612-2 | $9.99 US

Hex Vet
Sam Davies
Hex Vet: Witches in Training
ISBN: 978-1-68415-288-9 | $8.99 US
Hex Vet: The Flying Surgery
ISBN: 978-1-68415-478-4 | $9.99 US

All My Friends Are Ghosts
S.M. Vidaurri, Hannah Krieger
ISBN: 978-1-68415-498-2 | $14.99 US

Drew and Jot
Art Baltazar
Drew and Jot: Dueling Doodles
ISBN: 9781684154302 | $14.99 US
Drew and Jot: Making a Mark
ISBN: 978-1-68415-598-9 | $14.99 US

Space Bear
Ethan Young
ISBN: 978-1-68415-559-0 | $14.99 US

Wonder Pony
Marie Spénale
ISBN: 978-1-68415-508-8 | $9.99 US

The Last Witch: Fear and Fire
Conor McCreery, V.V. Glass
ISBN: 978-1-68415-621-4 | $14.99 US

Forever Home
Jenna Ayoub
ISBN: 978-1-68415-603-0 | $12.99 US

Jo & Rus
Audra Winslow
ISBN: 978-1-68415-610-8 | $12.99 US

Hotel Dare
Terry Blas, Claudia Aguirre
ISBN: 978-1-68415-205-6 | $9.99 US